THE NEW-CLASSIC S

SHORT STORIES FF

BOOK ONE

Zero 9-4

TREVOR WATTS

Dedicated to Chris Watts
For her editing skills, commitment and tolerance.

 The illustrations were all created by the author or adapted from free-to-download, or paid-for, images from the internet. Three of the stories have been included in the Giant Anthology of Sci-Fi stories "Of Other Times and Spaces", including "Kyre?" – adapted from the beginning of the saga trilogy "Realms of Kyre."

Log on to https://www.sci-fi-author.com/
Facebook at Creative Imagination

First Printing: July 2020
Brinsley Publishing Services

ISBN: 9798617570542

CONTENTS

BETTY

'Yike! Yurrrk!!!' I squawked. Choked. Spat. Had hysterics. Coughed, tried to shout. '—in my mouth!' Poking fingers in. Couldn't get at it, or rawk it out. Leaned over, retching. Felt it crawling. Still alive. Couldn't shift it. Must have been clinging on at the back of my mouth. I'm in a panic. Trying a last-resort tactic – to bite it – chew it. Crunch it. A live beetle in my mouth – at my throat. And it went crawling down my throat!

'Oh God, oh God, oh God,' I'm going, and looked around at all the wondering, ready-to-panic faces. I gasped, 'Damn-great beetle in my mouth… Swallowed it.' The thought of it inside me made me queasy, and curled everybody else's lips; and toes, too. I grabbed my drink. 'I'll drown you…'

Somebody at my table started asking daft questions, as if I'd deliberately eaten a massive great beetle. 'Yes, yes,' I was saying. 'Of course I remember what I was eating – the nyama choma with spiced tomatoes and ugali, with a half-litre of Tusker beer to swill it down. Not like you pack of health freaks.'

That was about the finest cuisine that Nguru Game Lodge could offer. The place was great for the big game, the rooms, staff, guides and the rest of the safari group. *But hygiene's a mite slack,* I thought, *there's a host of multi-coloured insects flying and crawling all over the open buffet. I must have swallowed the biggest of the bunch.* They kept a mini-flock of yellow-throat bee-eaters fat and happy as they went trampling all over the food dishes, spreading no-telling-what kind of diseases. Dozens of mud-coloured beetles skittered across the floor, and entertained the crested agama lizards as well as the guests.

'Rest a while. It'll pass through you. Eventually,' my well-meaning helper consoled. So I sat and felt wrung out, trying to sense if the damn creature was still wriggling. Very gradually, I calmed, with the help of a couple of Amrut whiskies. *I feel shattered. No way am I going out on the late afternoon and evening drive to the waterhole.*

All because of a centimetre-long silvery beetle that came crawling off the uneven raffia table-top onto the plantain leaf that the bread rolls were on. It stopped and seemed to look around for its next destination. Yes, it started off again. Smart, brilliantly silver in the sunlight, it headed straight towards me, and disappeared under the protective rim of my choma dish. Chic it might have been – glossy silvery carapace over its no-doubt folded-up wings, but who wants huge creepy-crawlies so close? One or two of the room staff were creepy enough.

I moved the dish out the way, brushed at the thing, saying something like, 'Bugger off, Tin-man.' It leapt up as the back of my hand went for it, hovered for a fraction of a second, and shot straight at me. I thought it was going to sting me or bite me in revenge for the half-aimed swipe, or general irritation. Straight into my mouth. Suicide mission.

I didn't sleep so good, having nightmares about massive praying-mantis-like monsters coming at me.

Next day, believe it or not, I felt better and worse in one. 'Well,' I said to the local maid, who spoke only Swahili, 'if it was going to poison me or eat me from the inside, I'd have noticed something by now – like blood and bits of beetle in the toilet.'

Better? Well – I felt fit enough to get up, wander round, nibble some nuts and fruit. How pervy do you get? Nuts and fruit! Me! Confirmed carnivore. 'Well, I am in Africa – maybe it's the heat, or an aberrant appetite. I expect I'm just not feeling like sausage, egg and bacon with black pud and hash browns – Kenyan style.'

Worse? I puked up over a beer at midday – I always have a beer at noon. *Always.* I have never been ill on beer before. The embarrassment. The shame. The two girls I'd been chatting up cleared off with two older women. *Women*, of all things, and my mate Jazzer was in the process of moving in with the young and rather smart carer of the old couple who have to sit at the front of the safari-bus.

Anyway. I was left on my own. On holiday. With a vast array of wonderful animal life outside, and a single gruesome specimen inside. The afternoon went appallingly. Wandering round, feeling extremely lost, bored and a bit queasy – the thought of that bloody bug getting mashed up and churned round and digested in my gut.

'Does the human digestive system cope with chitin, or whatever beetles are made of?' I asked the maid who had wonderful big brown eyes. I didn't really care – I'd perhaps absorb it, or pellet it up and spit it out like owls do.

I ordered a pint in the bar in the evening. Couldn't face it. Looked along the glass shelf of spirits; there wasn't a single one that didn't appeal. And there wasn't one I could face drinking. This was a bit of a downer.

'I like drink,' I told the Jambo guy behind the bar. 'I practice liking it a lot – on a daily basis, at least.'

You can see where this is going, can't you? Dead right – I couldn't look a drink in the froth for the whole ten days we were there. I say "we" were there, but it was me on my own. I suppose it was partly me being unsociable, but mainly them being miserable gits – drinking together, and whatever else they were up to. Except the batty old pair, I expect, but you never know. And, would you Adam and Eve it? I'd gone off every single food I ever enjoyed. I practically starved before I found rubbish I could face, and that I could keep down. Most of it was nuts, fruit and honey for the first four days.

'Bwana,' says Jambo the barman, 'you should try some local food off the buffets. All good things. Very tasty. Perhaps you like?' Thereafter, morning, noon and night I was grazing round the tables.

We moved over to the second of our "Two-Centre Safari" lodges. Different livestock at the waterholes and kopjes. Half the other guests went somewhere along the coast, and we collected five new ones. But a similar routine and guides, foods and drinks. The drinks, I didn't even notice – Lord-alone knows how, it's usually the first thing I check out. I define holidays as "Three-week blurs". The food? I tried a few different things – discretely spat a few into a tissue and took note of a selection of others, most of which I would never have gone within a table's length of before.

Before the second week was out, I'd found a reasonable selection of weird foods that I could face and keep down. 'I wouldn't stretch as far as saying I enjoy them,' I told the admiring couple from Batley who thought I was incredibly adventurous. 'I never look forward to them. But they're okay.' They remained impressed with my courage at eating "all that rubbish foreign muck".

Two girls among the new lot took a shine to me: 'You some sort of health freak? Are you?' That appealed to them. So I hammed it up a bit. Or fruit-and-nutted it up more than a bit, actually. So the last few days at Bisan Mwingi Game Lodge were quite a delight, to be honest. And I was fit – more than up for it. Or, for *them*, actually.

Tragically, they were going on to the coast for a week, and I went back home, feeling, to be truthful, not bad at all. Alright – I felt really fit. It was the flight back that was the real eye-opener: a total joy. Like I was in my element – and to see the landscape from so high! Wow! Why was I delighted? I'd flown before – *bor-ing*.

'Must be something to do with that Big SB,' I said. 'Silver Beetle. Must have been something powerful in its blood – or whatever beetles have. Maybe it's burrowed up behind my eyes, tapping into my optic nerve so it can watch. And never had the nerve or wing-power to fly so high before.'

*

'Bloody beetles buggered up my holiday,' I told'em at work. 'Put me off my food, they did – especially one that picked on me.'

They laughed, but Janey Wintershold said I looked better on it, and, 'How about the Dog and Donkey tonight?' That was a first. A night on Britvic orange and J_2O apple and mango was not the finest beverage occasion I've ever experienced, but Janey more than made up for it.

The yet-another-weird-thing was that I was looking at everything like I'd never seen it before – the kids in my class, driving the car, freezing cold rain, a hot fire at home. And at Janey – she'd never bothered with me much before, though we taught parallel Year Six classes.

The kids in my new class were fine – all in line from the off. That was a first – 'Yes, sir, no sir, three bags full, sir.'

I know. I had stray thoughts, like on the plane, but it was only later that everything linked up and it became totally obvious. 'It all dates back to that bloody beetle,' I confided in Janey, across the pillows. 'Something in it's messed about with my brain. Some chemical's tweaked me.'

'What chemical would that be?' she asked, not overly interested. She was busying herself with things under the duvet.

'I wouldn't know the actual chemical – that's beyond me.' But I could imagine some bombardier-type beetle having its last thrash round in my stomach, squirting hydroquinone and God-alone-knows-what in me and fusing my brain. I thought it best not to tell Janey all about that just at that moment: she had other things on her mind. Delightful young lady.

Except. I had this feeling that I was watching things – like studying my class, and the way I drove. I went swimming – that was traumatic down the leisure centre on Mansfield Road.

The way I didn't even consider alcoholic drinks was weird as hell at Christmas. And I haven't been near a Full English breakfast since Kenya. It was like I congratulated myself on it.

‘That’s disgraceful,’ I told my Aunty Maud, ‘The years I’d spent worshipping best bitter, and sausage, egg and bacon. It’s sacrilege to forsake them at the drop of a hat. Or flight of a beetle.’

Aunty Maud agreed and took the Mick – gorging on cocktail sausages and port all Christmas day.

You know what I decided then? My latest theory was that the damn thing survived in me. It had squiggled round somewhere inside me and latched into my brain or some such place. ‘It’s definitely the sodding beetle that’s doing more than just watching. It’s interfering as well, and making me feel de-fucking-lighted with myself and the world.’ Janey was accustomed to me talking about my imaginary internal beetle by then.

*

If only. That summer, shacked up with Janey Wintershold and thinking about a wedding, we decided to take a holiday – the Serengeti. She really wanted to see cheetahs. ‘Cheaters? You’ve got enough in your class.’ I told her, thinking of all the squealing and diving they’d been doing in the last football match.

I collapsed with a heart attack and burst brain aneurysm at the airport, just after going through Security.

Janey never forgave me, even though the insurance refunded the money. The wedding was off – she didn’t want to live with a potential corpse, much less someone who slagged off her class. They monitored me for four days in KMMC, and swore I was the most baffling case they’d ever encountered. They kept calling me, “The Handsome Case”. They even got my name wrong – I’m Alec Hanson; or Ally Kanson, as Aunt Maud says.

The docs wouldn’t be told. ‘You have all the symptoms for a heart attack and subarachnoid haemorrhage,’ they told me. ‘See? The X-rays and blood tests…’ And there was something about the troponin chemical things that heart attacks produce. But the holes and splits and swellings had sealed themselves… Self-repaired, whatever.

"Miracle Recovery" it said in the Daily Post. Even a half-minute spot on the lunchtime local news – they dropped it in the evening when something bigger cropped up – some councillor's road had potholes or something.

*

I changed schools the following Christmas and didn't see a non-regretful Janey after that. But that was okay – Maddy picked me up at a Christmas Eve party, and I spent Boxing Day and New Year with her, and her parents and brothers and sisters. I knew my beetle was watching and enjoying its first whole-family Christmas. It even let me have a drink – a toast to the New Year. I wasn't sick. I ate turkey leftovers and didn't vomit. I had roast pork and a glass of rose wine and survived.

Thinking I'd try an Easter break somewhere not too far, I booked a trip to Tenerife with Maddy, laughing that I hadn't made it onto the plane last time. 'Well, you needn't bother having a heart attack with me,' she joked.

Would that were all. I was just stepping into the twin scanners pad and my legs wouldn't move. I begged and forced and damn-near cried. So Maddy went on her own and came back with a tan and a positive pregnancy test.

Thus, I concluded, my beetle doesn't like powerful X-rays. It was enough to knock me out. Yes, I collapsed at the airport again on the way to Morocco at Spring Bank. The public side of Security this time. In the hospital again, and they put me through the MRI scanner. Oh, boy, did that wake them up. Magnetic Resonance Imagining. Magnetic. Jeepers – my beetle was pissed off at that. It showed up. That little silver sod was still there alright – bedded on my heart. With its nest. And tiny beetlets scattered all round. 'I'm a bloody colony,' I wailed to the radiologist. 'These things – the size of poppy seeds – are in my blood.'

'They don't appear to be doing any harm,' said Mr M'Wolla, the consultant. 'In fact… we can't really tell what that mass is. It's not cancerous, so we'd better leave it alone. Don't want to risk a mass spectrometer to find what metal it's made of. You think it's a beetle? Unlikely. You haven't been shot, have you?'

*

I can travel on planes if I show them my Medical Risk Exemption Certificate and/or submit to a strip search. So we're not limited to the UK. Been all over, actually. That worried me for a time – Am I seeding the world with silver baby beetles? I don't worry any more, because I must be. But so what? There's nothing I can do about it. Betty guides me, with a rod of chitin – That's my joke for the day.

Twenty-eight years, it's been, without a day's illness, and I look the same now as I did then.

Another thing that used to bother me was the way I kept looking up at the sky, day and night. Not to admire clouds and stars, but as if I was looking for something. 'Are we expecting the Beetle Mothership soon?' I used to tease her and smile, 'From Betelgeuse?'

I have the impression that Betty, as I think of her – The Beetle from Betelgeuse – doesn't like me saying things like that. Bit too close to home, I reckon.

She seems better about it now: she's communicating more and more, and it's much clearer, more distinct. We're both quicker to pass the discourse back and forth. Lordamighty! It is *so* weird – gaining an understanding with a beetle. A sort of internal messaging system.

Betty seems happy to know that there are about a hundred English-speaking countries in the world. Satisfied that will be enough if we don't spend too long in each one.

It's a pity I haven't had a stable relationship since we met. I don't know why. I like women. Really like them, and I don't get the feeling that Betty objects. But it never goes any further than a few months, a year at most. I can't imagine why I have no children – there's been enough sex to start my own school. I would have thought Betty would want lots of us spreading the word. 'Maybe I'm infertile?' I asked her. 'Or are you not of a maternal bent?'

We still look up more than most folk, but not as intensely as we did at one time.

'So maybe the Mothership's been delayed. Has it?' I asked her pointedly one night when we were watching out for the Perseid meteor shower. And I waited for a reply from within. I mean – *very* pointedly. And waited. Patiently, like I expected an answer. Demanded an answer.

And I received one. Not a couple of sentences, nor even a beetly nod. But a definite affirmative blip in my head. 'Soon?' I asked. And waited. I didn't know beetles could shrug, or be disappointed. But that was the distinct feeling I received from Betty.

'We're on our own, then?' I sort of stated and asked all in one.

That elicited something in the nature of, 'Maybe.'

'I'd rather like kids,' I said. 'They'd be company.' But received no response. 'You must have millions of them.' I pushed the idea, but it fell on stony ground.

So maybe all her tiny poppy-seed kids don't survive – perhaps she's as childless as me.

*

I have a feeling that this is going to be an *extremely* long-term relationship. I'm thinking Betty got her calculations wrong by a few zeros on the end – like a factor of a thousand or so, with regard to the arrival of her companions. Not *five* years; more like five thousand.

I'm picking up the vibes that she's content to wait, and prepare for The Coming.

Six times I've changed jobs, and worked in three schools, and in three unrelated research areas in three different countries. Betty seems to like research; she has an enquiring mind. I've changed my name twice, just to see how easy it was – complete with new identity. At the same time, I tried a persona change – to be a different sort of person. A bit quieter and more serious. Next time, I'll try a few eccentricities for practice. I think I need to build up a repertoire.

I'm getting the distinct impression that I may well need all this expertise.

My age and my eternal youth don't appear to put the ladies off; and I'm sure not figuring on going off *them*.

BIGMOUTHS

Our flight was delayed, so we were marooned for an overnight stopover on the Hub Port orbiting Planet Exxen. No private room to settle into, so the spacious lounge area it had to be, with ten dozen other stranded souls. It was tolerable but I found a trio of rounded tables next to one of the huge panorama windows. 'Settle yourselves here,' I told my little group, 'and I'll fetch you a trolleyful of snacks and drinks.' I'm like a real mother to them. I expect it's my feminine charm. 'There's a variety of foods from the four main planetary systems hereabouts, and drinks from half-way across the cluster. Now then, any specific preferences? Okoi... okoi... one at a time...'

I took their requests. 'Back in a couple of shakes of an Obci's ding-dongs,' I said, and left them to enjoy the terrific views of the dawn light spreading across Exxen, five hundred kay below.

They were quiet enough when I returned; beautifully-behaved, in fact. Politely helping themselves to the stacked-high treats-trolley, and relaxing calmly in the face of the inevitable. 'We'll be gone on the morrow; until then, let's think of it as being free of care, hmm?'

Others around the lounge were snuggling down, their flights the same – delayed or missed or over-booked. Kids and families, party types on holidays; business groups or a henty party; and singles here and everywhere of all hues, shapes and tentacle counts. From planets dark, or moons so bright they'd burn your eyes; oceans of silver, or airborne clouds, the stranded passengers in this multi-lounge reflected them all. We had a quiet little game of seeing who knew which was who and where from. And how they managed to breed – but I had to put a dampener on that direction after a few minutes.

Just one pack was living it up. 'Nerves pre-flight,' I kindly assumed. 'Ignore them.' I hid my distaste well, I thought, as the new arrivals drank and smoked. Became louder, more lubricated, some folk edging away from them. They were enjoying the scene they were creating. One in particular was all mouth. All four mouths, actually. Tentacles everywhere, touching up the humans on the far side – the males *and* females. BigMouths thought it was hilarious, all the shock he was generating. So did his gang of Hulker partiers, all girly giggles and frilly squiggles.

Oh, yes, a right laugh… they egged him on. More hoosh. The bar manager tried to close off the drinks machines. I didn't hear the threats, but he went white, then green, and backed away – left them to the hoosh and smokes, and us to the mercy of the Hulkers.

'It's going to be a long, long night,' I said to my little lot. 'So just stay relaxed, hmm?' But it was going to get worse. All of us in that lounge could see it coming. You only had to gaze around to see it writ on every face, every melancholic mandible, every shivering shellcase and fibrillating pharynx.

Sure enough, free to rampage, the Hulker party-group began fairly gently, but escalated swift as Baldrican with a bare backside – bullying a group to join in with their "singing", which turned into a compulsory striptease show for their own delight. Not even the same species – they had no idea what it meant to the Jadeans to be naked in front of others.

Or for the Tewdys to be forced to drink alcoolish beverages – it's downright dangerous for their metabolism. But, it's not up to us... Heads down, mind our own affairs.

Their attempts to sexually assault a group of Madeni proved to be a mite too much for them, however – the Madeni being, as you know, semi-metallic clone-breeding entities, with the non-metallic half being largely ethereal pseudo-matter.

Someone dared to find their efforts amusing. I imagine they wished they hadn't, when they found they were paying the bill for the Hulkers' drink, food and smokes, plus a few additions from the duty-free shop.

We kept our heads well down, my little party and I. I told them to. And they do as their Surro-Mum – as I think of myself – tells them. And they're my *family*, as I always call them when we're travelling – my little boys and girls. This was no occasion for them to be involved in. But BigMouths, lording it over the Hulkers and everyone else, knew a born victim when he saw one – anyone half his size, apparently. Like me. And I'm considered pretty big at home, on Karlik. As well as quite pretty. So, with a certain inevitability, we eventually watched him drunkenly tottering our way in hundred-deci-belch ominousness.

Tentacles stretching threateningly over all our heads, and frills erect – the randy toe-breakers – he and his Hulker cronies half-surrounded us in our little space by the vista windows. The night view of the occasional twinkling cities below was to have been our last view of the planet – probably still would be.

My little group of ladies and gentlemen – all from Susuu – it's only me who's from Karlik – stayed beautifully, obediently quiet and subdued. 'You are good little souls,' I told them. *'Despite everything.'*

A probing tentacle came seeking down at Lolly, my dainty little one with *such* blue eyes. I could not permit this to happen. 'Please desist,' I asked BigMouths. 'They are my responsibility. More than that: I am *totally* responsible for them. Kindly cease doing *that*.'

As BigMouths took growing courage from dominating a family group of quarter-his-size Susuus, I considered the situation. I'm responsible for their welfare and safety: I know it, and they know it. They look to me for support – Lady-Mack Bethy, as they call me.

I mean – my Susuus are squidgy little things, wouldn't harm a fleeg, or say "Boo" to a goonberry tart. Totally harmless – couldn't possibly offend anyone. Why on Buzzock would BigMouths, Gropicles and Droopy-frill want to pick on my harmless little group – and me?

This was not something I could understand; or allow. I stood, and he laughed. 'Mini-Squidge,' he called me. *Me!* That is even more not-on. Even more not-on than picking up two of my tiny charges and rubbing them together like he was trying to mate them, or make them burst into flames.

So. I simply had to act, before this all got out of tentacle. You know how it is – they're *My Charges*. My little Susuus. Out of several corners of my eyes, I could see others around the lounge watching. Probably certain they were going to see us all dipped in the shampy fountain and nibbled on. 'My friends,' I began to address BigMouths and Riot-Party, 'let us not be hasty. Please put down my young companions. They do you no harm. You're drunk and know not what you do.' I like to quote the Kuck of Bells: it shows I'm an educated girl.

But would he have it? Or any of them? No, they wouldn't. Grabbing Milly and Pensivalle and sucking at them – they're all slime and slobber, you know, these Hulkers. 'Okoi. If you won't listen – Coo-ee! Suzies!' That's my call sign for them to pay close attention. 'Effective immediately, twenty years off all your sentences if you find a Hulker to exchange identities with. I'm switching your restraints off... *Now!'*.

My lovely little Susuus heard that alright, though BigMouths' gang wasn't listening to anything.

It must have been a wonder to behold if you've never seen vids of Susuus in action before.

In three minutes flat – staggering, limping, sagging and seated, as well as flat – the exchange had taken place. Pits! They are *something*, my Susuu Convicts. Little jewels. *Fast?* They could rip the tentacles, mandibles, palps and proboscises off an elefundrum in ten seconds: they really could. The Hulkers didn't stand a chance.

***

So here we are, basically. Still waiting for the connection and deciding to have a little drink. My former-prisoner-Susuus are very quietly celebrating with a single drink each. Showing off their new identities as neoteric Hulker holidaymakers with Fun_Stars.orb. They seem to be quite proud of their huge ID discs and docs. Each has a sample of Hulker DNA as their ID proof – mostly a tentacle-tip or a pedium, but I think blue-eyed Lolly has BigMouths' gonads.

No-one in the lounge has said anything about a dozen vicious Susuus being freed, with Hulker passports and free transport to Modrigau. No-one else is travelling to Modrigau, so nobody really cares what they get up to there.

Nor does anyone appear to be upset about a dozen newly-inducted Susuus sitting silently with me, each supremely obedient to the call-signs I control them with. I don't imagine the prison camp on Vlaudox Two will care that the batch I deliver to them isn't exactly what they were expecting. They probably can't tell the difference between one way-out prisoner-group and another – Susuus or Hulkers? Who knows? Who cares?

As long as they do their twenty years with good behaviour.

CLEANUP

'Jerry, you remember that planet collection that Yoiky made when he was little?'

'And we couldn't find where he'd put it? Yes, what about it?' Jerry costumulated his zyfroags rather nonchalantly.

'I found it, I think. Changed a bit from what I recall, though.'

'Oh?' Jerry looked up from his quasaring with little rustumial interest.

'Mmm – He had those lovely gas giants in really close orbits round the star, so there was all the flaring mass interchanging and really spectacular. It was very good, for a little lad, anyway.'

'And? What are you getting at, Belinda?'

'They've moved right away from the sun now, and they've gone cold. I'm sure they're the same collection. One's got all little bits round it now, and the other has these awful-looking rings. And the other beautiful big ones? They've been moved even further out and they're completely frozen.'

'Sounds like somebody's been messing with them. But, if he will forget where he put them, what can he expect?' Jerry couldn't really be bothered with such pirrinking things when he was attempting to micro-manage an infundibular structure in Co-Lossus T. But Belinda was clearly in an asmorric mood, so he divided his tenticular burbages, 'What's nearest the sun now?'

'Some rocky little things – you remember them?'

'Not too well; it was a long time ago. They were fairly much the same size, as I recall? Just different colours? He picked them up from some systems we passed through, coming out of Galactic Centre? Are they the ones?'

'Yes, you *do* remember, Jerry. Anyway – one's gone all dirty rusty red; and one's gone cloudy. Another's so close in and very hot where the gas giants should be, and the other one's gone soggy, with blue and green slime all over it.'

'Yeuk.' Jerry felt obliged to respond in some sympatho-auricular manner, although refilling a black hole was infinitely more interesting – literally infinitely.

'Exactly – Yeuk.'

'I seem to recall there were more? Some smaller ones?'

Yes. One's got itself locked into a close orbit with the mouldy slimy one. Or somebody put it there – bit of a delicate placing, that. And the others are all over the place. One's broken up – or did Little Yoiky screw it up in a temper when we had to move on?'

'Well, whichever, what is it now?' Part-saticated with the progress on the black hole, Jerry could listen to Belinda's witterings again.

'It's just a great heap of bits littering up the central part of the system – quite untidy. So I was wondering: it's Yoiky's five-billionth birthday coming up soon, and I thought it might be an idea to tell him I found them again?

'Shouldn't bother. He's ignored them all this time. Never mentioned them again. Sounds like somebody else's been playing with them, anyway. But, if you must, I'd clean them up and put them back where they belong – you know, gas giants innermost – clarify the cloudy one, polish the rusty dusty one, wipe the slimy mould off that third one.'

‘That’d be a lot of bother. Can you give me a—?’

‘No. I need to spend quality time wikidiking with a magnetic banding anomaly just the other side of Perigassius.’ He diverted an attention spectrum to Belinda again, ‘Yoiky was never that bothered. Just leave the bloody things alone, unless you’re going to do a *proper* job of cleaning them up and re-arranging them right.’

‘I’ll see… I might have enough time this post-sidereal.’

DONYA'S TALE

Our little craft – The Moonlight G – was perched there like a cockroach on a Kalėdas cake. Obvious and vulnerable. In the middle of a bare rock plateau a mile diameter. We were as exposed as we could be.

Even I felt vulnerable, personally, and I wouldn't be a target for anything. I'm merely a support lady – an observer, interpreter, translator. I don't have a specific role in the actual negotiations, other than to watch. I'm Donya; I'm a Reader – it's what my name means in Allegaic.

If I'm asked, I tell Her Serene Majesty what I see, or hear. And smell, if it's the Ghasuls we're with: they convey a lot of their meaning through aromas, and they don't realise that some of us can interpret it. It's not like I actually need to go up to Her Serenity and whisper in her ear. She can touch into my mind, and I can send vibes – mental alerts, and our team hear them like a quiet voice in their heads. It's not only Her Serene Majesty I can communicate with through the vibes, it's anyone who's approved – and today, that's everyone on our little team. But I never ever vibe to the other side. We don't want them to know, do we? I just read them.

'Mmm, you're a super-useful lady to have around, Donya.' Her Maj often tells me that, and smiles. 'So up your game while we're here, hmm? I need you to be on form.'

'Yes, Serenitya,' I vibe back, knowing she was simply giving me a heads-up reminder of the importance of the occasion. I could have said, 'Your Serene Majesty' but we weren't in the Negotiations Hall, so we weren't quite that formal yet. And to use her actual name was utterly unthinkable – I cannot even bring myself to think of her given name, much less ever to use it. She is *Her Serene Majesty* – in gold letters, capitals, underlined, Empire script, and neon-lit. She is the Embodiment of All Humanics. She is no longer a person, a frail human like me and everyone else. She is *Her Majesty*.

But, when we're mind-sharing, in home territories, unceremoniously, she quite likes the informality of allowing me to think of her as "Her Maj". Nice, that. It brings our thinking closer together – in synch. Quicker, more accurate.

So we're sitting here waiting. For our hosts to see we are here and unaccompanied. And for our opposition to do the same. Then, if they trust us, we can meet, we can talk. Negotiate.

Two hours we sat there on that bare rock plateau. Two hours! While the Xaw took their time on turning up! And we're sitting there, in a barren landscape of deep, deep shadow and brilliant stark light. 'That damn sun is like an arc light, but cold.' Captain Scoate said. I don't know what an arc light is, but I conveyed broad agreement back to everyone – just warming up our links, really.

In they came, the Xawaare, while we sat and watched them swooping in, circling us twice in tight turns. Acting it up. *Three of them!* Totally against the agreed rules. 'There should be one ship,' Peace Commissioner Aulde said. Rather indignantly, I thought.

'They're supposed to arrive in a single passenger lounger, like ours. Not the latest version of lightweight destroyers.' according to the mind-feed from Captain Scoate, 'Showing us their big guns, hmm?'

'At least we're all gathered together now,' Her Serene Majesty said. Serenely.

The servants of The Watchers joined us on the landing area when the other craft were settled, and they escorted us into the Great Palace that had been selected for the Peace Conference. Our arrival in relatively unfriendly territory was complete commitment to our desire to resolve the issues with the Xaw, and our respect for The Watchers and the Xawaare. The Watchers had made all the arrangements – so everything should be perfectly equal in the treatment of all.

We walked into the Royal Hall. And straight through! No refreshments. No cordialities. We were being escorted as though we were dangerous, or prisoners. Her Maj! *She'll not be happy about this, any more than she had been about waiting out there in the full glare.* I could tell that without peeking into her mind. I was latched out of her thinking at the moment, anyway. Not that it could ever occur to me to chike through the cracks of her thoughts. Strictly off the moral counter, that would be, with any of our delegation. And unbelievably especially not with Her Serene Highness.

All the time we were walking from our ship, and through the Royal Hall, she was *so* serene. That much was obvious, purely from her demeanour – her smile, her walk. Her eyes might convey more, but I walked a pace behind and to one side. I know my place.

Then, when we arrived in the Negotiation Hall, the affair went one hundred percent down the slippery. *The Watchers should be organising this whole matter – following all the conventions, everything. Ensuring total fairness of treatment to both parties. Observance of rules and politenesses.* Even mild-little-me was shocked. *They should not be doing it like this. The Watchers, of all people!* But it's not up to me to react. Only to observe and report on what Her Majesty asks or probes for.

I was registering it all – The Xaw Dictaro was so insulting. He ignored Her Majesty's extension of her fingertips to touch in greeting! Ignored Her Serene Highness! And she didn't react at all. She is so calm. So serene. What Majesty she personifies!

He called her "Kio". It means "Dearie". OmiUnoWhat. I hope Her Serenity doesn't realise that. And he walked away! Or bandy-legged squiggled away, anyway.

Then. We're in the Negotiation Hall and we pause and turn to them, give the ritual bow. Except they didn't return it! They simply stood still. Their senior was vibrating his sensor-palps. Worse and worse! That's the equivalent of a condescending smirk. I feel Her Highness flicker into my mind, an enquiring touch.

I knew – it wouldn't be going down well with Her Awesome Serenity – I knew her too well. The epitome of control, she was and always is. Serene is her title; Serene she is. OmiWord, she's everything. Humanity in Perfection.

A touch in my mind. A tendril touch to give her access to all I thought, for my observations and analyses; my impressions of the occasion, the referees – The Watchers who see that all is fair and adhered to. The adversary, the Xaw, emanating their self-considered strengths and smirks and cowardly bows. I read them all and leave my analysis wide open for Her Serene Majesty to read and delve, and quiz me about if she feels the need.

The Watchers stood by as the Xawaare dignitary ignored Her Supreme Serenity totally. It was deliberate – his palps frilled slightly at the tip, for just a second. He knew she was the leader of our party. He turned his back on her. A huge, fully-intended insult, I relayed it. Her Maj received, absorbed it. The Xaw turned back to us. He nudged her elbow – He touched her!!! Moved her aside! An airlock-expulsion offence, at the very least! He gives her papers to carry – like an aide! And points to a low-table seat – like a secretario! His exo-sac dangles in view – OmiGodFathers!!! All so massively insulting. And worsening! – He places a flag plinth on the table of the Xaw – there's none on ours: they're not allowed. He sat down before Her Serene Illustriousness was seated. *This'll not go down well with anyone* – it's beaming wide to everywhere – the Humanic Commonwealth as well as the Xaw and here in the Neutral Realms where The Watchers live. This is totally deliberate insultation and attempted humiliation.

I stayed back, as is my place, and detected the tension in the shoulders of our male-team as they stepped forward to their indicated seats at the front table – the seats clearly lower than those of the Xaw, and even the so-called Watchers – *those treacherous curs.* I shouldn't think such thoughts, but they knew it themselves. I read it in their Rachnid minds; they weren't being equal to both sides here. And all I saw and interpreted was open to Her Maj to read.

I noted it all, filed it, 'Let us all be aware,' Her Serenity conveyed to me. 'Leave your analyses open to all our team, my Donya.'

The Xaw and The Watchers, of course, have no idea that we can do this thing.

She sends me a glimpse of her inward calm, her fury cold. *Precisely what I expected*, I saw in her mind. This didn't bode well.

So calm, serene, Her Majesty, she let them talk and insult, and state their increasingly outrageous demands. They think they're victors here, and we're too weak to put up a fight, so obvious to me and all our folk. And anyone who's watching in on the UniCasts will know the same.

And The Watchers, the arbiters, are bowing to the Xaw! They're unaware that I can read inside them, know them, can read their outward feelings that even they cannot help but portray to the worlds. As though on display to me, I see the hundredth of a second intake of breath of the spiracles – that was well-disguised disapproval of what the Xaw just did, but they continue to allow it. The fractional loosening of the lower mandibles... Oh, yes, that was actual shock – must replay my observations to see if it was shock at the Xaw's ignorance, or at Her Serenity's – well, serenity. They knew it was wrong, but were giving in, letting it slide. Their cowardice.

The rest of our team say nothing, of course – we exist to support Her Serene Magnificence. It's she alone who is in charge. Yet here she is, at a side-table, alone, as if cast aside by the Xaw. So obvious to all who watch and see the shame they heap on her. Our team, at the forward tables, stays silent, as indeed they must, while the Xaw state and demand and threaten. They browbeat the Watchers. Glare their frondules across at us, in our lower seats. Or I was standing, actually. I prefer to stand, for the better view of other participants, and there wasn't a seat for me. Anyway.

We listen. We speak little. Me, not at all. I analyse their expressions and words and gestures; can detect some surface thoughts. And I file them all for Her Majestic Serenity to access.

She raises a hand, Her Serene Majesty, and stands, smiles in tranquillity. *We understand the position exactly now,* she conveys to me.

And so does all the Commonwealth, I think it back, *and all the Xaw and Neutrals' Realms that are looking in.*

I detect her tiny smile – *Oh dear,* I think.

'Many thanks to all,' Our Team-man says, as he rises, too. And bows to The Watchers and the Xaw who frill their palps and smirk at us. *You've opened our eyes and those of all who watch. We now clearly see the extent and depth of your greed.* I read in our spokeman's foremost thoughts. He smiled and repeated our thanks.

Her Serenic Majesty brought the meet to an early end. 'Many thanks. We understand. We shall respond in the passage of time.'

She turns. I stand aside and wait behind. Our team arise as one and nod in silence to The Watchers, and follow her. The Xaw are left, bewildered. The Watchers, too. I see the spark of light catch on the glitter-plates of their thoraces. *That means they flexed a heart muscle – which means tension – and that means lack of knowing – which they don't like.*

Yes, Serenity, I send, *The Watchers realise what the Xaw have done in their insults. And are ashamed that they allowed it; were not the impartial referees they should have been.*

'A1.' Her Maj mind-sent to me.

'A1.' I relayed to the commander in our ship.

'A1.' She passed to Base.

I paused and waited a moment, listening for the reply. It came seven seconds later. 'A1 enacted,' I confirmed, before Her Serenity and the team were half-way to the slowly-opening doors.

The only Humanic left in the Hall of Negotiation, I stood still, awaiting Her Serene Majesty's next move. It came. *Ask the Watchers if they will kindly accompany you to the vid-screen lounge.* Her thoughts came to me loud and clear, serene as ever.

'Yes, Serenity.' I turned to them, slow and calm, as is always my way. I bowed, and smiled to the Watchers. My! Their thinkings – They were bothered, worried – anxious, even – knowing they had permitted too much social latitude from the Xaw in the formalities. And all being broadcast cluster-wide, too – I see the redlight beams – still transmitting live for all to see. To see their fairness? The equality and equanimity of the proceedings? The just demands of the Xaw? The weakness of we Humanics and the sham of our Commonwealth?

'Would you like to...' I requested their presence in the observation and communications lounge. Puzzled and slightly anticipatory, they came with me. 'Not exactly the unbiased arbiters, are you?' I vaguely beamed in their direction, with Serenity's permission to give them a hint.

The three Watchers who caught my thought paused in their steps, fleetingly glanced to each other. *A pang of guilt and foreboding,* I detected.

Scarce a moment in time, we were in the lounge, the wall ablaze with lighted screens. Her Serene Mightiness had assumed complete control of the room. And the halls... the palace. *Tell them,* she conveyed to me, and I turned and repeated the words that came in my head, 'There is a total communications blackout. No-one leaves. Our Battleweights on peripheral patrol will stop any attempted departures by anyone.'

'What's going on?' The Watchers were a mix of confusion and concern. 'What are you doing?'

That was rather sweet of them – to suddenly decide to be a touch worried.

'We are clearing out the Xaw bases on Rihg, Tensor and Maig. They are *our* planets and have been for over a century. We no longer tolerate Xaw incursions there. Any Xaw ships in our realms are being taken or destroyed, including the three ships that brought their delegation here in an unwarranted and illegal show of force. That in itself is an act of war. *We are ending that war.*' I quite enjoyed saying that, and studying their reactions. My Word – Yesss, they were palp-vibrating-concerned now. Desperately so.

'Clear them out? Does that mean…?'

'Yes. Her Serenic Mightiness has sent out the A1 order—'

'What?' Their bewilderment was so intense I bathed in it. 'A1? What does that mean?'

Tell them, came permission from Her Majesty.

'It means, literally, "Bomb four shits out of them."' I indicated the screens on the end wall as one of our team changed the connections. 'See. It's being done now. The Xaw invade our territory, demand possession rights. And we agree to allow you Watchers to preside over our discussions. And yet you allow a palace-full of insults to be heaped upon us – our humiliation being broadcast live, hmm? Well, Watchers, you can now see how we Humanics react to insults.'

'But, but…' The Watchers watched, their horror mounting as results came in – a ship exploding soundlessly against a starry background… Their three grounded ships de-powered on the pads. Bases and communities on Rihg being entered, evacuation enforced.

One base was resisting, and swiftly disintegrating. Every screen displayed a different scenario of doom for the Xaw. All going live down the Watcher and Xaw channels. Their duplicity revealed.

Her Serene Majesty spoke, 'I am the embodiment of The Honua Imperia; Starpoint of the Humanic Commonwealth. To insult me is to insult all our peoples, our planets and territories, our sovereignty, our rights as people equal to any others.

'*Nobody* calls me, "Dearie".

FRIDAY NIGHT IN SOMERCOTES

'Is this Somercotes?' this guy in the car park asks me. 'I'm an alien.'

'You don't look much like an alien to me,' I says. 'But it's hard to tell round here, especially on a Friday night.' The sights you see when you haven't got a gun, eh?

'No, no,' he insists. 'I *am* an alien.'

'Yeah, and I'm your Aunty Flo. You know, "Go with Flo, your local pro". It's my working catchphrase. You interested?' I tease my blouse open a bit. No bra.

He gives me a funny look.

'Half price, if you're an alien?' I offer. Well, trade's been a bit slack, even at my prices.

But he just mutters with this weird little mouth – like my younger brother Joe's. 'Gottle of gear, gottle of gear,' or something like that.

'Look mate,' I tell him, 'I seen better than you on Stars Wars, and that must be a thousand years old. I'd have thought modern alien suits would've come on a bit.'

But he's going on in this metal voice. I mean – who does that these days? Not since the Daleks and that science nerk in the wheelchair. Only his voice is getting screechier, like metal grating. 'Good effect, that,' I tell him. 'You need to work on it, though. 'I mean – if you're alien, you'd be going like, zipperdeedoodahzipzipzipzip54321, wun't you? Or in binary, like 111000111. Stands to reason you ain't gonna be talking English. I mean, even Surly Sid from Newcastle 'an't got the 'ang of English, 'azi?'

'I travel through this region,' he says, all shiny and two heads. Them heads! One lurking behind the one I'm talking to!

'Come off it, Binary 001, I can see where the join is; it's all wrinkled. And your eyes! Yeah, right, you're definitely off the planet Zoggle if you think aliens have eyes like that. I've seen'em exactly the same at Partymask.com. And if you hang about till closing time in Alfreton, they get loads just like you. If you want to do the alien bit, don't talk with your mouth – Aliens got to be better organised than that. Just don't talk out your backside. *Everybody* does that round here.'

'But I *am* an alien; I'm passing through.' These four antennas come out of his back-facing head and swing round, like studying me.

'That's a good effect,' I congratulate him. 'Just passing through, eh? Looking for your mates in Pinxton, are you?'

Then his antenna-things grow and swing round me, like sniffing. I sniff back, 'You smell sort of acid-sweet.' I poke at one that's nudging into my blouse. Mucky little git. 'If you're really an alien,' I says, to put him off, 'You'll have a todger three foot long, bright green, with grappling hooks on the end, won't you? So show me.'

And he did! And we did! In the car park next to the Chippy. Ye Gods! This is gonna look so good on my CV.

GO FOR A WALK, OSCAR, DEAR

'Go for a walk, Oscar, dear. It'll do you good. Just fretting round the house all day, you are…'

Heaving myself up, she was right. I ought to get some exercise. Perhaps the rain had cleared away. I looked, 'Maybe.'

So I went, taking my usual route through the village, over the stream and into the woods, taking the winding, overgrown track up the gradient through the trees. Muddy underfoot, and pushing the overhanging dripping twigs and leaves away, I was getting soaked anyway. The thick misty damp in the air didn't help, and certainly wasn't doing me the "good" that Mari had promised me. I was getting plenty enough exercise walking all the way up here. I had my camera at the ready – flushed with the success of having two of my photos shown on the telly as a backdrop for the weather forecast.

It was only another two hundred yards, at most, to the top of the slope, the footpath rough and rocky in places – the result of heavy rains and neglect. I turned left when the path levelled off, just for a change and a challenge – a little more exercise along the rising track wouldn't do me any harm.

The old mineral line was up that way, and there were several routes back from there. Yes, why not? That way would be fine.

I arrived out of breath on the trackway. It was the final climb up the steep embankment that tatered me – the steepness, and the rough climb where there used to be thirty or forty steps. Now collapsed, and more overgrown every time I come this way.

Still breathing heavily, and waiting for my heart to come down to normal, I looked up and down the length of the old track – the rails themselves were long gone, but the ancient line used to run down the ridge from an iron-ore mine and smelter higher up. Still mostly clear of undergrowth, it was possible to see a good distance in both directions, left up the track to the site of the old mine, and right, down to the river.

The whole edifice was pretty substantial, the height and length of the rail line, beautifully graded to ensure a very smooth descent all the way down to the barge port that carried the iron ingots to the foundries and mills. 'Must have been a substantial mine to make it worth building a line as solid as this,' I scuffed a boot at the slate and cinder surface that steadfastly refused to give good rooting for the rosebay willow herb that swathed the patches where the trees didn't create too much shade.

From here, I usually took the right turn down to the river, but… for a change in this misty, clinging weather, why not take the other direction this time? The walk was only gently upwards – the wagons would gravity-roll down here, centuries ago, and not *too* fast, or they'd have shot off the end and cleared the river completely.

Yes, a pleasant, easy stroll. A few photos of a squirrel, couple of blackbirds… long-tailed tits… Until I reached the end, where a massive spoil heap completely blocked the whole track and spread for a hundred or more yards to both sides. Not from the iron mine; this was from a stone quarry that was worked after the iron had petered out, or ceased to be economically viable. For near-on a century, the stone quarriers had removed a great section of the upper part of the hill. It was unfortunate that their cast-off tailings had buried all trace of the iron workings. There they were – somewhere under there, under a million tons of stone slabs and blocks. It was partly grassed over, with bushes and saplings, but much of it carried full-grown trees – more than a hundred years since the last slates had come skittering down these slopes. The huge heaps and banks were merged into the rest of the landscape now.

I stood, at the base of the first and highest slope of waste stone, letting my leg muscles recover, as well as my lungs – unaccustomed to this kind of uphill distance walking. Getting my breath back, I thought I'd take a couple of pics if that green woodpecker was somewhere around – I'd heard it tapping a couple of times on the way up here. The wild garlic aroma was strong in the air… and I should be able to get some really atmospheric views down through the trees, across the misty fields in a couple of places where there was a gap in the trees.

'Rest here for a while,' I told myself. 'Take a pic or two… circle back via the picnic area, and be home in time for tea. Kate and Sidney pud, as I recall Mari saying.' Not so much a circle as a triangle: up to here; down the track to the stream, then home via the Stone Bridge and Headstocks – both fine hostelries.

Squawk! Clatter! Squawk! Squawk! Flapping, cackling, thrashing in the branches immediately above me. Birds squabbling. A rookery up there in the higher trees, huge shining-black birds that had lots to say sometimes. I raised the camera in case I caught a glimpse of anyth—

'Oscar? Oscar?'

I've always loathed that name, been ashamed of it. Seventy years of wishing I was Mike or Pete or Alec…

I looked. Mari, my wife – she shortened her name from Marigold. But Oss wouldn't make a good shortening for mine. A white and cream room. Bare walls. Hospital, obviously. 'What are you doing here? What am I doing here? Am I in…? Whafor? Mari? Mari? What's this? What's happened? Heart attack, have I had? Stroke? Where am I?'

'Queen's Mill, Love. In the ICU. You had an accident.'

'Eh, what sort of accident? Lord, my head hurts. What? Branch break off or something?

She was holding my hand and looking so relieved, and concerned. She's a jewel. 'A hole in the side of your head – like from spike or a pick axe. They think it was a bird – a huge rook – that flew into your temple, just above your left eye. It split the bone, went really deep and pushed some fragments inside. Oscar? It's been weeks, nearly three. They didn't find you till next morning. There's the rookery just there. Feathers all over the place… A dead rook nearby. And black feathers in all the blood. You lost a lot. You were at the bottom of the old steps. Looked like you'd fallen from the top – covered in blood and bruises. Like domestic abuse, they said. Looked at me a bit funny, too.'

None of that could I remember. Just instant nothing from lifting the camera. To waking up a moment ago. *Three weeks?*

'I was dreaming.' I said, images swimming into me, moving. All around me. I was among them, part of them. Yes, I was dreaming… 'I was gone back years and years, Mari,' I mumbled, the shifting visions swirling and closing in around me; sounds. 'It was like the iron mine and the foundry were working again, and I was up there in it. They had a smelter up there.'

'What?' she laughed, 'Under that great spoil heap?'

'Yes. I know. It sounds daft. But it was so real. The quarry waste wasn't there. It was the original trackway. The carts were being used… running past me along the track. I was walking along there, up the line to the foundry. It was a big wooden building like stables, with the top half of the walls open.

'I could see inside – crowd of men in the darkness – a fire glowing in there. Then I was going in, and it was a smelter – a furnace. I could see inside this black-iron opening. Blazing yellow-white light. And a furnace there. So hot… *so hot.* I was near it. People all round me, smelling of burning and smoke and stinging my eyes and nose. Grimy men, women and children in canvas clothing, rags, or long leathers. Some staring at me. Unloading coal. Shovelling it into the furnace… red-brown ore into the smelter. Some women were pushing carts further through the building to what looked like another smelter…

Lots of kids… Donkeys and ponies pulling and pushing. So busy. I was like battered down by all the noise and a really acrid smell… So noisy with clanking and shouting… grunting and cussing. Really loud hiss of scalding water right next to me. Made me jump and there was steam and feeling hot all over me.'

Mari had that baffled-but-patient look she reserved for when I'm rambling… Like most days. 'And you were just wandering round in this dream? And nobody noticed?'

Did they? I thought, remembered. 'Yes. Yes, they *did* notice. Some children came up, asking something, all big-eyed and smudged faces. Coming and touching me like they hadn't seen anything the same before. Asking me things. Wondering about me. And so was I. And I don't think I was answering, and they were getting belligerent. Thought I was after something of theirs.

'And then… then…' I tried to think. Next… Yes, 'Couple of men came pushing through, and a great hulking woman with a shovel. She was the worst, threatening me. "Begone… begone…" she was right in my face with it… and jabbing my chest with her shovel.' I felt… yes… could still feel where she'd rammed it at me.

Mari looked puzzled. 'The doctor said you had some bruising there. It'll be psychosomatic, I bet.'

I could feel exactly where she'd pushed me. 'Some girls came round me. Pretty. Laughing at me, feeling my clothes as though they've never seen the like before – See, it's got me talking the same. One of them actually said that, "Never seen the like before." They were in work rags… Heavy clog shoes. "What are you?" they kept asking, as if I were an apparition come among them.'

'Have a drink, dear,' Mari reached for the water jug.

'They started pushing me, shoving me away.' I could feel a sweat coming on now, just to recall it. 'It was so real. Frightening, really. I was trying to say I was Oscar. I was lost… visiting… not spying or interfering or whatever they thought. "Demon," one of the men said. His face was all snarly and angry. Some others were coming at me. Pushing me. Throwing things. The men and the women were crowding round me. Really angry about me being there.'

Lord. Even now, in bed. Everything clean and white, and Mari with me, I feel scared – my heart going like the clappers. 'I remember I was staggering round among them. Couldn't get away… knew I needed help. Really panicking and I was gasping – so hot in there and so panicky, saying to let me go… leave me… not hurting them… Hitting at me and I kept stumbling.

'Then they'd all gone from me. Suddenly gone. Ignoring me. They were all round the smelter. Something needed their attention and… and…' I let Mari sit me and plump up the pillows, give me a drink.

'Careful, Oscar, your lip's swollen a bit, and you've had stitches. Must be from when you fell and rolled down the embankment.'

The dream was still in me, all a mad panic in my mind, remembering how I'd gone cold, and been running to get away. I was outside. And all the kids were round me – filthy urchins, like savages, throwing things. Hitting at me with these things like rakes and hoes, but heavier… a spiked thing – must be tools from the smelter, or raking out the furnace. Lordy-dee, Mari; it was so real. I can still smell that place.'

Jeez… so *real*.

'That's how dreams are, Oscar Love. You're in them. You live them.'

I was in Queen's Mill four more days. Then they kicked me out. About time, I was feeling so restless by then. Needed to be somewhere familiar, among my own things.

I still have trouble getting my balance, and I need a walking stick even round the house. Eating's a bit of bother – can't seem to get my mouth chewing properly.

The hole in my temple still leaks watery gunge and I have to keep dabbing it. So I spend a lot of time indoors – and I get irritable-restless. Thus, I've had time to catch up on organising and editing my photos from the summer – two holiday folders from Lanzarote and Turkey; a fun flight in a bi-plane; a cousin's wedding in Hucknall. Plus lots of the flowers and birds in the garden. And loads more from days out – Chatsworth… Scarborough and the coast. And the same again from my morning walks, including half a dozen folders of pics still on the camera chip.

I loaded them all on my PC, just folders with the camera's date code and number…

Even some from the day I was injured. The folder said it had sixty-odd files inside. 'I don't recall taking many pics that day. The camera must have got its knickers in a twist over the date.'' I clicked to open the folder…

View – Extra Large Icons.

Squirrel… blackbird…

The first pic on one row was a wooden cart on the wooden line. Two children were pushing it on the next pic – looking scared; looking at me. I know my mouth was drooping open.

There was a view down the line; the rails stretching away along the treeless slope, two other carts in sight. The twin rail-line stretched up the slope to the left as well. The pic that way was wonky, like I'd not pointed and focused properly. The great grass-and-trees spoil heap was gone… the top of Stoney Hill was recognisable in the background. More people working at the carts – men in leathers, hoods, cloaks. Hammering at hot iron… an oversize barrel of hot ash or clinker being raked. Some unloading timber. Others coming out a mine entrance.

To my eternal shame – there was a selfie. Me – looking idiotic – *and no blood on my face;* with the iron-works building behind me.

I scanned through the other photos... fresh heaps of red and black iron ore. A giant smelter, half buried into the solid ground of a steep bank. Smoke and fumes – I remember the sting in my eyes and lungs. Red-hot pigs of molten iron beginning to cool. Yes, I'd seen those in my dream.

It was all there. I recalled the sounds, the voices, a donkey braying. And subdued clunking, a loud roar. Someone chanting time... the rattle of cart wheels on stone slabs. A man shouting. Such deep shadows inside, and the furnace so bright. Everything so alive and real.

I just stared and watched as the vivid images sequenced through again at eight-second intervals – the first dozen were of birds and squirrels. The other forty-nine were of the iron-works. I needed a drink.

'They *can't* be real,' I was insisting to myself, 'Somebody's messing me about – having a laugh. I mean, folk in the old days were all grainy, and black and white. They *must* be fake, mustn't they?

HOLDING ON

I always donate to the Solar Rock Rescue Team. There's a collection box in the Stellar Bar – the scruffy one at the cargo transfer base that orbits Palless, not the posh-for-passengers one at Space Central. I was in the workers' bar – the "characterful" one, on a day-and-nighter with Middy, who I sometimes ship out with, and we drink together whenever we happen to meet up. 'You never know when you might need rescuing.' I touched the credibox for ten percent to go to them.

'You hardly ever see their teams in bars or anywhere around the ports,' she said, making her point by looking all round the bar – low lights, lots of swirly smoke, stinking of gar-weed; mostly humans, couple of tourist diffies from somewhere out Neesia way. They come here for the experience of a rough-mix bar.

'And you pray you never need to see them out in the bebs.'

'Huh?'

'The big empty black stuff – don't you know anything?' We always take the pick out of each other. 'Keep up with the lingo, Midds.'

'Two percent tax on all space-goers' earnings is plenty enough for me. I don't give no more.' She nodded wisely and sipped her kee-wing special.

'Yeah, well,' I said, 'It's fine by me; and so's the fifty-percent of cargo value for any rescue and recovery. It's never my ship, or my cargo.'

'So, it's a service that you've already tax-paid for. Don't see no reason to give'em more.'

Dayve, the loading master for the cargo base, came over and joined us. We all get on okay with him. You either get on well with him or he screws up your next load. 'Middy's right, really, it's practically free rescue for crew who don't have any share in the voyage.'

'Especially crew like me.' Being a load handler and stacker in the cargo hold, my basic pay isn't enough to pay huge amounts of tax. 'Anyway, it makes me feel better, like I'm doing my bit.'

'Right,' they both eyed me up like I was a Knutt.

'Like I had this one-year contract aboard the SS Mary Q. There's only me doing the hold-master job during the voyages, and I spend most of my time in a suit, 'cos the skin's a bit leaky back there in the ship's hold. It's big and dark and prone to infestations of astro-fungus.'

'Yeah, tell me about it.'

'So sometimes I have to gas it out with a one-day fumigation.'

'And you have to stay in there, in your suit? Gets kinda claustrophobic thenabouts, don't it, with all the green gas smoking round you?'

'Yeah. Eerie. It semi-condenses in the cold – cargo holds are always cold, and have this sort of cavernously silent echo… Well, you know how holds are unless they're full to the airlock. At least the danger money bonuses are good; and they're not taxable.'

'Sure,' Dayve semi-sneered, 'like you've ever actually earned your danger bonus, huh?'

'You think spending twenty-thirty days alone, mostly in a suit, in a leaking hold, having to gas it out every few days isn't dangerous enough? Koh, if it's your shout next, Dayve, I'll tell you about the last time I was hold-mastering the Mary Q.'

'Mary Q? Little old freighter on twin drives? Big scratch along the port side? Remember her.'

'She wa'n't that little. Ten-thou-tonner.' *Little? The Mary Q?* I was affronted. 'Anyway, you know they call it "holding on" when you're locked in the cargo bay during a longish voyage. You're praying nothing goes wrong. And the flight crew're hoping you're okay and keeping up the maintenance on heat, perishables, hull splits, fraying cables and the like. Not supposed to be alone for more than twenty days on a trip, but it happens when there's no way-stations, or somebody's paying double for a *Now Delivery*.'

'It's the way it goes,' Middy philosophised over the drink.

'We were heading out on the far fringes of the Ganiton Cluster looking for somewhere called The Hyton Base to deliver whatever the cargo was – machine parts, most likely, for a drilling and mining operation somebody was starting up.

'I was hearing over the comms system there was a HyMAG storm in the area—'

'That's a hyper magneto-gravitic force-field?' Dayve didn't know everything.

'Yeah, screws everything up,' Middy helped out. 'That's pretty much what the "Hyper" bit of HyMAG means – it makes a hyper mess of you.'

'So, of course, I imagined Cap and Navvy would be replanning to avoid it, and I just carried on as usual back in my domain. What else was I going to do? Everything was routine till there was this tingling everywhere, and the lights cut. The air-con slowed down, and there's this crackling in the air. So I slams my face-plate in tight and waits. And waits. Nothing. A blast of the HyMAG must have swamped through the ship and caused a total loss of power on the main engine. And I'm thinking if the others are still alive, they'll be trying to fix it and get us back under power. But there was nothing – internal comms were dead, no hammering, no more engine vibe. It had sure done for us.'

'No power means no engine; equals no control; equals no chance. Y' never told me y' had bother like that in the Mary Q,' Middy was a touch miffed.

'Y' never bought the drinks before,' I joshed her. 'Anyway, down in the hold, there was nowhere for me to go. No internal communications – lack of battery maintenance, I imagined; or the circuits overheated. Whichever, I couldn't leave the hold. You know how it is, I'm fairly solidly sealed in for the whole of a voyage, anyway, with my own air supplies, survival cubby and snack cabinet. And I was totally vacuum-packed in there by the loss of main power.

'I thought we had the side impellers working at one time, because I heard slight sounds and vibrations through the metalwork. No hammering, though, so I didn't know about the other crew.'

'How many? Cap, Navvy and Engineman?'

'Yeah…' Bad to think back on it. 'It's lonely, uncomfortable and risky all the time, anyway, but, like I say, the money makes up for it. But when you don't know if the others are still with you, it's lonelier and a lot more uncomfortable.

'The actual conditions in the cargo hold were no worse than usual, but being completely cut-off isn't nice, with no chat times, no sign-offs, no popping through the inner lock to the lounge. It was dead, like that, four… five days… and I was getting kinda bothered—'

'I'd have been suicidal,' Dayve was all ears and empathy.

Middy's fingers slid over my wrist. I thought she was trying to stop me drinking, but it wasn't that. 'Shit, Myki. You should'a told me before.'

'Yeah, well… I'm trying to busy myself, not think about things, checking the pipes and cables same as always— I suddenly get this whirring. Feel it in the plates. Side impellors starting up. So sudden. They don't do that on auto, so somebody else had to be still alive, and was trying to do something. I tried the screens. The hull-inspection cams lit up—'

'Same power banks as the impellors,' Middy nodded.

'So I tapped in for a panorama of the outside, and there was a tiny point. I was getting views of it every nineteen seconds, swinging down the screen, so I figured we were in a slow roll-over. And we were moving sideways towards it. So Capn and/or Mate must be up and about, trying to get us there.

'It took a day to get a decent view. Some no-atmosphere rock heap of a moonlet that was rotating end-over-end, and at about the same pace as we were – which is hugely fast for a trillion tonner asteroid – but its roll was at right angles to the Mary's. 'This is gonna be awesome. Us with one rolling vector and that thing with totally another.'

'Ain't no way. And y' still here?'

'Yeah, just about. Then it was closing in fast. Weird, seeing nineteen-seconds-apart views of this thing spinning across the screen at a helluva rate. I'm feeling the impellors on and off every next second. So somebody's doing something. So close in then. Nothing more than a rockscape racing past. Completely filling the screen. Must have been slowing, cos we stayed real close for maybe three rolls. But there was no way we were going to avoid collision with it. And a trillion tons of jagged rock isn't going to stop spinning for a ten-thousand ton powerless cargo vessel.'

'They just sort crumple up – the ship, that is. The rock don't get more'n a scratch or two. I seen a wreck they brought in one time. Wasn't even scrap – just some high-val cargo.'

'Right, thanks, Dayve. Anyway, Mary Q was so close – like almost within its topographic level. We'd be swiped by a passing pinnacle at any sec. Them rock peaks were hurtling past, and we were still spinning.'

'That'd be something – smashed and bounced back into space. Or smashed and sent crumpling across the rockplain till you drop into a canyon. Shite, Myki…'

'I heard the impellor going, practically roaring, trying to steady us, match speed and spin. It was impossible for something our size, and already way out of control. It's one way to go. You know how it is – I decided years ago that if I was ever marooned I'd wait it out as long as poss. Some guys have opened up their air-valves or cut the heating elements so it happens quick. But I'll hold on if the worst comes. That's the real version of "holding on".'

'Like it's the *real* man's way? Yeah, right.' Dayve wasn't too plugged-in to that image.

I gave him the rock-lubber look and carried on, 'Strapped in, buckled down and holding on to everything I held dear, I braced up real tight. First impact was out of sight of my little screen. It shook the Mary like— I dunno, a million hammers going at the hull. Shrieking and metal tearing. We nearly stopped dead. Huge lurch and roll. Another… Another… Cargo splitting loose everywhere.'

'Y' were rolling?'

'Kinda. And that was about it. But, Cap'n had got her down, must have almost matched speeds at the last second. *Crash*-landed, crumpled, rolling onto her side, and finishing damn near upside down but I was still alive in my suit, and cocooned in the cubby. And the screens were still lit up – half and half black space and grey rock. Just the same, we had landed.'

'I need a drink,' Middy said, looking pointedly at Dayve.

'Koh, right. I will. When Myki's done.'

'Damn damn damn… I was cursing and pulling and pushing at everything in sight, and still couldn't get answers from whoever else was aboard. Took me a couple of hours to re-jig the battery connections to the emergency beacon – but it was already broadcasting our location, so I added my own "Condition and situation" message to the emergency one. And sat back for half a day's wait in the cold and dark, refilling my suit air twice. I had it all worked out – I had eighteen more days food and drinks, which might see me through. The air, on the other pipe, was only enough for six days. And that would scarcely be enough for the signal to arrive anywhere, elicit a response, and for anyone to travel here.'

'It'd depend on the value of the cargo, I reckon.'

'Right.' We all knew that much.

'So that was a bit of a downer for the rest of the day. No responses from hammering on the internal bulkheads. Nothing from the internal comms for another two days. It was already pitch dark in there – three mounted dimlights all faded away not long after we'd finished rolling. And it was getting real cold as well.

'At least I wasn't getting tearful and ranting about it. I always knew it could happen, years ago when I first came on the freighters. I'd had a better run than a lot of cargo guys—'

'*Zeedle-eep.... Zeedle-eep... Zee...* Oh f'! I was whirling round. That was a Relief beep. Coming over the rad! Could hardly breathe; I was just gasping. Di'n't believe it. Then I'm watching the HI screen for any sign— Yes! Yes! I get a glimpse of a craft spiralling past and out of sight. Right over us. Must have seen us. So I'm waiting... "Come on come on come on where'd you get to? There! Yes..." Shytit, I was up the moonspout. This Solar Rock Rescue craft came in like a rocket—'

'It *is* a rocket, Myki.'

Sour-thicko look in Dayve's direction. 'It comes weaving round to match orbital speeds with our moonlet, no messing. Right on the edge of my screen. Fantastic control, like a gymnast doing triple spins and a double back-flip. Perfect, light-as-a-feather landing in the boulder field next to us. "Jeeby-doo!" I'm saying. "You guys are *good* with a capital udd. You'd put Capn in the shade eleven days a decca in any craft." Real demon that pilot – true Ship Jockey, he was. Or she – a lot of pilots are women.

'Another half-day wait, and I'm going, "Are you even looking for me? Know I'm here? Finding the others first?"

'Then I get this tap tap tap... Tap tap tap. It was them. Coming round the hull. Tapping and radding on the exterior. "Great! You found me." Extraction in no time – They're cutting a sodding great hole cut through the shell. Then they had to shift a thousand tons of cargo out the way. It only weighed half a ton there, but its mass was still pretty awesome, and it took some moving to get at me in my little survival cubby. But they must have been used to that kind of thing, cos next thing I know, I'm being heaved out and I'm tottering across the dust to their ship.'

I needed a big drink, just remembering it. Bad time then – me rescued, and finding the others... Well... They hadn't made it intact. Freddy the Engine had been hit when the motor blew: his top half was vaporised. Then when we hit the rock, Cap hadn't had a suit on. He said years ago that he wouldn't hold on. He'd get it over quick. Probably never thought we'd be rescued. His lungs had haemorrhaged a mite and cooled right down – a minute or two. Navvy had his suit on, but his legs were crushed. Still with us, though. Just about. I was okay. Just stirred-up, and still shaking. And filled my suit once or twice.

'Not that the Rescue crew cared much about either of us: we were both on a freebie trip, thus of no particular value, beyond fulfilling their obligation to rescue all personnel, or they don't get rights to half the cargo. They pointed me to the cleanup cubby and set about assessing the logistics of recovering the cargo, and placing "Claimed-so-keep-off" beacons on the Mary Q.'

'That's the most important part of it for them, I reckon,' Middy knew the way of it.

'When they were finally ready, they fastened Navvy down in the sick box – like a glass coffin. Invited me up to the crew's flightroom for a screenside seat – all of us belted in and watching the screens. Tight little room, padded seating. A dozen all-round screens.'

'Bit different to the Mary Q, huh?'

'Sure was. All shine and efficiency. "Hey," I says, "No console? Pilot?"

'They pointed to an oval door through the rear bulkhead. "In there. I'm merely the deep-space Captain," the guy in the uniform said. "Me and the Navigation Officer leave landings and take-offs to the expert – she's a specialist Harbour Pilot. Brilliant at this tight inner manoeuvring. You see us come in? On a landing as awkward as this spinning mess?"

'So we sat and watched the screens, "Hold on," somebody called. Next sec, we were pressing down into the padding as we lifted. Fast - and on a spin. Whoever was back there doing the piloting, they had all the poetry of a motion genius. We were off the rock in a zip and spin, hover, point and go. All in one fluid operation.

'I asked who it was... "Someone I've seen round the ship?" I said.'

'"The pilot?" the Captain said. "No, you've probably not seen her. She's in the command cabin, hooked in, wired up, and head-setted into the whole motor system, navigation banks, impellors and balancers. Her mind feeds directly into the cams and controls that feed the screens."

'"Total instant control? Just for the close-in manoeuvres? We never even dreamed of anything like that on old freighter-crates like Mary Q." I told him.

'"It's the only way we can get in and out of tight revolving spots like these; they shift unpredictably.

'"There," he says. "Looks like we're in the clear already. We'll swap over shortly, when she comes out. We have a direct run for home from here, unless another casualty beams in on the way, of course. We've been warned this could become a Long-Period Patrol if these Hy-Mag-storms don't subside soon.

'"Hang on," he said. "I'll go and unclip Jasmine. Joe E, our regular pilot, can take the rigging now we're on the easy bit."

'The pressure door eventually hissed and swung open, to allow the Harbour Pilot's egress. I *had* to see this woman: the Ship Jockey; the Enter and Leave Harbour Pilot. Somewhere up there with God on her right hand.

'Out she came. She was beautiful, stretching long and lean. Front, then back; arching for a quivering moment. A couple of strides, a purr and nudging the Captain, a quick damp paw across her whiskers right and left.

'Cap'n reached to her, "Ready for milk and a fish-bake treat, eh, Jazzy?"'

'The pilot was a cat?' Middy and Dayve said it together.

'That's exactly what I said. And the Captain said, "Of course – have you ever known a cat to cock up any take-off or landing? You saw us coming in, didn't you? Whether it's six feet off a windowsill or ten thousand off a mothership, they *always* land on their feet.'

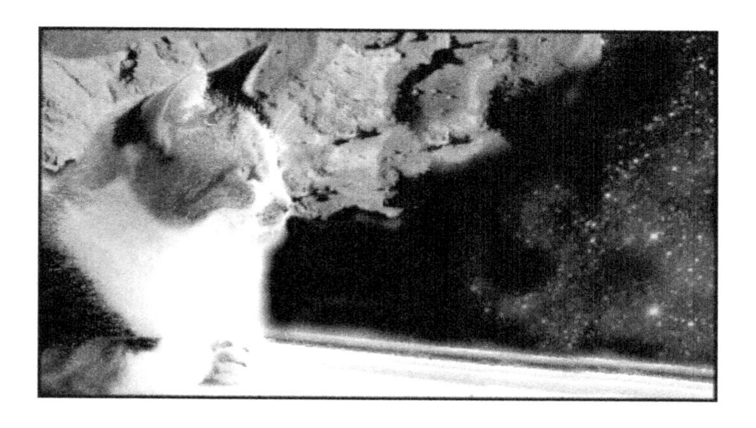

IN YER DREAMS

'I sleep alone. I sleep soundly. I do not toss, turn or masturbate too violently.'

I told the doc that, so it's not a dirty secret. He was going to ask me, anyway. 'Best to volunteer information sometimes,' I tried to smile at him, but that wasn't too easy since I'd woken up with so much pain in my right arm. Till he prescribed oxy-codamol. Then he spoiled it by admitting he was mystified as to how I'd shattered my arm in bed. 'I'm sorry, Ms McKenzie. I'm a junior doctor in A&E, not a detective. I can tell you fairly precisely how serious a spiral fracture is, and predict the prognosis for its progress. As to how it occurred…' He spread his palms. 'I've no idea *how* you could sustain a twist injury such as this whilst asleep. Perhaps it might help if you could calm your mind, and think yourself back into what you might have dreamed of. Can you do that? I can recommend a hypnotherapist.'

About all I heard of that was the last bit – something about pissed – which I felt.

The best of it was that I went out with a nurse-bandaged arm that felt moderately comfortable and warmly numb, after a double starter dose of the pain-killer. But also with a very disturbed mind that pricked me with whirls of faces and struggling limbs. I couldn't make sense of any of it.

'I can't drive for five weeks.' I wailed to the taxi-driver. 'I broke my arm in bed.'

He gave me a very knowing smile.

‘Piss off,’ I told him. ‘Keep your eyes on the road.’ And went back to recalling a few black-hole nights lately. Totally blank, dead nights – you know – passed-out-in-an-operating-theatre-type dead periods. Usually, I dream for ages. Long, complicated dreams. I sometimes recall fragments, if I make the effort. But who has the time to do that? Busy busy busy. Work and all that crap.

Like there was one a couple of nights back: I was in the glass and metal offices at Glynn & Sons, and they were being devious and smarmy, and I flounced out and couldn’t find the way. Like a glass maze, all red like in the sunset… and a huge foyer – I remember thinking they’re just showing off with a foyer like that – a lagoon in the foyer! With palm trees! And Sunset! And I was running all over the place trying to get out, and thinking I’d have to swim in that red lagoon. And I did and came out the other side and didn’t have my clothes on and the only way then was back into the glass offices where *they* were waiting… Made me shudder to think of them. I know there was more, but I can’t get into it. *Creeps.*

My mind’s never at rest. Of course I dream a lot. That’s normal. Just lately, though, some nights have been these absolute blanks, like everything’s-been-wiped clean.

Reminds me of all these memory sticks I have with tons of folders and files and notes on them. And then I come to one that’s been re-formatted – nothing there whatsoever. That’s my head some mornings – totally vacant.

I must have been muttering – Uber-man was smirking again. I growled and said, ‘One more snigger from you, and it’s no tip.’

Doc had told me, ‘You should rest for a week; use that arm as little as possible.’ That was on top of the driving ban.

‘I haven’t got time to take a week’s rest.’ I was aghast at the concept. ‘I don’t overwork. My job satisfies me. I couldn’t sleep without it. Couple of days over the weekend, maybe, with my arm aching so much. Can you prescribe gin to go with the oxy-codamol? I’d be alright then.’

Then he had the nerve to ask if I was being domestically abused. ‘Twa— er, *Twillop*,’ I told him. ‘I don’t do domestic.’ I can summon up a really withering look sometimes, though.

But I have had some really rough days when I’ve dragged out of bed feeling as if I did eight rounds with Tyson Fury. There was one time recently when I looked in the bathroom mirror, and I had a right shiner coming up. By the time I was into work that morning, Wendy’s nearly dropping my coffee, ‘That’s a one huge swelling there, Jillian. Blue and yellow already. What you been—?’

‘No idea.’

She laughed. ‘Looks like you’ve met a violent dream-mate.’

‘With Jill? Chance’d be a fine thing, eh?’ Bertha the Hippo joined in. Uninvited.

‘Yes, well. We all know about *you*, Bertha.’ She received my extra-chilling look.

And there was the time, just last week, when my legs were knackered – jelly all day.

‘You were all jumpy and edgy the Monday before, too. Dead nervy at the least little—'

‘And that time you said you felt utterly shagged out—’

‘Yes, thank you, Bertha, for reminding me.’ I’d sort of buried that one, when I needed the day off to bath and shower and scrub down cos I felt dirty all over, like mauled and groped and… and raped. I had a couple of bruise patches on my boobs, and my legs, and… down there.

Thinking about it in the taxi… *Yes, it's getting too much. There's something up with me, to be doing this to myself. Or maybe it's someone getting into my home? But no-one has a key, and the windows and doors are all bolted. And the chimney never even lets Santa's little helpers in, much less Big Boy himself.* It was beginning to get to me… more than just wondering and shrugging it off. I mean – a spiral fracture can be serious.

'You're extremely lucky it's not far worse,' Doc had told me. He also mentioned psychiatric help.

That was when I called him something else not very nice, but he said, 'It might help, Ms McKenzie, whatever direction it might lead you.' And he gave me an extension number of the hospital; said Dr Szieter was a friend, 'I can give him a ring, if you want?'

So, thinking more about it in the taxi… 'What the hell.' I rang the extension. Doc One from A&E had already had a swift word with him. 'If you do want to see me, I have a cancellation in half an hour. Can you get in so soon? Where are you?'

'Effin great,' I said. 'I just come from there and I'm outside work now. I'm going to have to be nice to my Uber-guy.'

I allowed Uber Wan Kenobi one more smirk, seeing as he was okay about it, and he even took me through the hospital grounds to the psychiatric wing. That was when he smirked.

Waste of my time! This "recommended" psychiatrist bod pondered and ummed and couldn't decide anything.

‘You’re a waste of space,’ I told him in my flounciest-possible tone, and headed back to work. On the bus, no more taxis.

I’m settling nicely at my station – the big one because the floor boss always has the biggest desk and area. But Mr D’Alba from Human Resources came to see me. He did the H&S as well, and seemed more bothered about making sure I hadn’t done it at work. ‘Fret not,’ I told him. ‘I was in bed. You must have heard. I’m okay. I’m trying to concentrate on this Westcliffe project.’

‘Just the same, we have access to a hypnotherapist—’

‘Not you as well? The hospital was on about that.’

‘She’s in today – been very helpful – Dave Threll in Maintenance who was terrified to go in the basement? Marjory Cripp in R&D stopped seeing grasping fingers coming out her computer screen. And I learned to cope with my fear of being up here on the fourth floor. She’s very good. I could probably get you in this afternoon? Her diary isn’t full.’

This was all too much. ‘If she’s as big a waste of time as the Psycho…’ I warned him.

I never thought I went under, but she seemed sure I had, and we talked about it after. The gist of it told me nothing new: normally, she could “break into” recent memories and dreams, and dig around the edges, unearthing feelings and suchlike. So these bits I’d told her about – the arm, and bruising and jelly-legs – should have expanded and filled in, at least to some extent. ‘But they’re a complete blank in your mind, Jillian. It’s as though the whole night, on each occasion, has been removed.’

‘Reformatted,’ I helped her out. ‘It’s what I said when we started.’

‘Very much so. As though surgically removed.’

‘The hospital must have some kind of deep brain scan that can reveal abnormalities in me?’

‘CT scans and the other equipment can’t see into memory holes, tangles and buried thoughts, I’m afraid. It’s more *if* you’re thinking, not *what* you’re thinking. But,’ she busied her little grey head, ‘one could reveal if there are damaged areas. I’ll see what I can do… Who was the psychiatrist at the hospital? And the A&E Doctor?’

Isn’t it amazing how they can fit you in when they’re actually interested in “your case”?

Next morning, I was all wired up with electrodes, injected, and connected to screens with squiggly lines and bleeping patterns. They showed me pictures and patterns, and asked me lots of questions – some relevant, most silly and pointless. They played some music – loads of it in short snatches; and videos – I remember a dog on a beach… soldiers running with guns… Oh, yes – and some smells – perfume… vinegar… farmyard dung. And something to taste – salty crisps… and chocolate… Not Cadbury’s, though.

‘May we touch you?’ One asked.

‘Careful,’ I said. ‘There’s a dozen of you and you’re not all having a feel.’ I watched very closely as they stroked my hands and feet. And even had me running my fingers on what felt like sandpaper… or silky hair and stuff. Then they were back to touching me on my stomach and hair and cheek. I freaked out then. It was so weird – I was getting these images and thoughts and feelings, all racing and jumping through me, and dashing and crashing in my eyes and my head.

They got me calmed down, and did some more – carried on for ages, they did, in a rota of people and machines. Like I was a little student-project for them. Then somebody took me to the canteen where I could have lunch and they'd see me in their suite at two o'clock.

'You're very interesting, Ms McKenzie. Exceptionally. Allow us to explain…'

'Er. Actually, we *can't* explain what's been happening to you.'

'And that's very interesting.'

They showed me some screen-drops and prints and graphs and grey blurry pictures that I think they said were inside my head. I'd have been worried if I'd known what all the differently-shaded bits meant.

'We're not entirely certain what they show, or what they mean.' Senior-type doc told me, and she was telling the others as well, in her best Gestapo voice. This was clearly the official version *vitch you vill stick to, unt say nothing more. Underschtood? No Schpeckulation.*

Yes, they got her message and stuck to the authorised line. They did try to explain it to me, but it was more of a wondering discussion among themselves.

'These graphs have unusual aberrations…'

'The cortical scan has several particularly rare highlight areas…'

'There are blank spots here, the like of which I've never seen before outside a cancer-filled head.' That was the fill-em-with-confidence Chinese one.

'They're black spots… holes.'

'That's what I said they were. You're adding nothing to what I already know.' Huh – doctors.

'It is as though these black areas are physical as well as mental blockages... almost with a barbed-wire fence around each one – as if the conscious mind was prohibited from going there.'

'Certainly, Ms McKenzie, your responses to some touches were extreme to the point of hysterical.'

'And other stimuli prompted similarly intense reactions...'

'One might say near panic-stricken.'

'Clearly, you have acute anxiety about a number of specific sensory inputs – particular images, scents, touches...'

'Well you would be too if—' I burst out. And silenced on the instant. *Oh my God! I just had a flash of—something.*

They carried on, partly explaining to me, partly trying to explore with each other, then back to asking me... and re-discussing...

I was on another planet by then... Er, no, not really. Not literally. But I'm sitting there and getting these flashes... Seeing *them.* All this scanning and talking had woken something up – like being in a dark room and there's suddenly a dozen camera flashes within a second from start to finish. Like you might get a split-second memory of a dream and then it's gone.

This was a dozen all at once. And they hadn't quite gone...

I need to be out of here. They're all talking at me... I got to go somewhere quiet where I can grab at these fragments before anything gets in the way, like somebody saying something that triggers something new and it wipes the old...

So I was on my feet and leaving. 'Got go. Need to think. Remember.'

I think the rather smart James Bond-type doc realised what was happening and he said, 'Let her go,' when I thought they were going to try to restrain me.

I sat in a corner of the canteen and stared at the trio of potted trees in front of me... seeing faces snarling and laughing and hearing voices... feeling myself running or struggling... shadowy people coming together... The running was before the jelly legs and crawling and laughing faces. I'm staring at the green plastic conifers, but they're a hedge that won't let me through to remember more. It was changing into a wall, and I'm seeing images of men... in rough working clothes. They're laughing and we're in a game of some sort. It's a black metal sheet now, but I see shapes behind it and feel hands, hear music. Something thrilling inside me... then frightening me so much. Nearly wet myself. I wonder if that was the morning when the bed was wet?

I saw things happening in flashes – like windows being lit up for a fraction of a second. It was scary. Really scary. But coming together, in strings, joining into events, complete dreams that had been fragmented and buried.

'Are you okay?' One of the docs was sliding into the seat opposite me. It was him, the dishy one who said, 'Let her go.'

It was getting late – they'd be closing the canteen soon. I was so jumping and sweating I couldn't talk to him till I'd sorted my head out, so I had to go, and I caught the bus back home, except the connection wasn't running and I had to walk the last couple of miles. Nearly had a couple of bumps into other pedestrians and took the wrong way twice, then dropped my front-door key, and had to sit down when I made a coffee, and topped it with Irish cream.

All these bits were coming together. Untangling the threads of ten different dreams at once. No – more like making ten dream jigsaws at the same time, from a scatter of pieces that kept arriving. I was getting long periods when I was running along lanes and tracks and over fields; being hunted like a fox…

Another… Someone had hold of my arm and I was screaming to escape and they were forcing and yelling and my arm was twisting. I think they were trying to stop me doing something, but I was in a panic and my arm took the brunt of it.

And that time I'd been bathing and showering all day… I really can't re-live the reality of that one… can't make it come back again – the most humiliating. No – I can't go back there. No wonder that was blanked out my mind. Except it was back. Six… seven… eight of them? Men laughing and mauling and treating me like a kickabout jelly ball. Raping me…

I poured a double gin after the coffee and cream, seeing it all, realising – They *did* do it, and they blanked it out my mind. Why hadn't I cottoned-on before? Lord I can be slow sometimes. So obvious – somebody was getting into my mind and doing things with me at night – not every night, but maybe once or twice a week, or month. My twisted arm and the bruises were psychosomatic – enforced imaginations. But they'd been real… real to me, and the fractured arm was real enough to the bods at the hospital. And had actually happened, but can't have been physically. Can it?

Someone can get into my mind so clearly and so intimately that I live their fantasies – or their actual realities if there are several of them?

Another gin, and stuff the tonic.

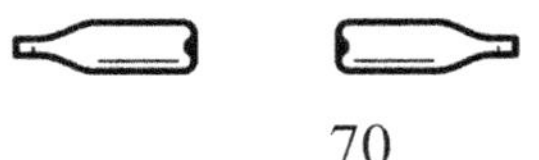

By the time the bottle was empty, I was wondering: Will they realise that I know? Would it make a difference to them? Probably: they must have a reason for completely blanking me. They surely can't be on another planet? They'd felt like just people. From the future? They'd be risking it if they were – doing all this to me might change things in the future and make themselves not exist.

Or someone from the past? Some weirdo Victorian inventor? Maybe it's some kinky-pleasure sado-masochism thing that some pack of pervs have got going? Am I being rented out to any passing deviant shithole?

If they know that I'm aware of them now, am I going to catch a glimpse of a sign-off message saying they've been rumbled and better drop this one? In which case... *how many more sleepers are they accessing?*

'And,' I asked the replacement gin bottle, 'how do I join them? That doctor is really *very* good-looking. I could do a few things with a body like his.'

INCIDENT AT MUFFLETON BOTTOMS

Time: 0800 hours: Sheriff's Office, Delmonica County, Philadelphia, Penn. 'APB. All 10-8 officers. BOLO for groups of rednecks converging on National Rifle Association rally at Conestoga Park, Phil. Known bunches heading in from Pittsburgh. High likelihood of disturbances along highways and back-routes, especially from the west. Maintain high profile in pull-ins – keep berries and cherries lit up. Establish vehicular checks along all major routes into the city from the west. In the interests of public safety, warrants have been issued to apprehend the following individuals and vehicles…'

Time: 1306 hours: Daisy-Mae Dixon was clearly re-living the whole delicious nightmare. 'First we knew, Sheriff, there's this lumberjack guy, size of a grizzly comes bursting in. Straggly yeller hair all over him, "Willy Joe Deacon, that's me!" he's yelling. "Yuh kin tell ya friends y' met me, in the living flesh! And you-all gonna jes sit back and keep yo little selves quiet while me and the boys…" And there was this whole bunch of'em just burst in. Ten of them. Microbus-full. All drunken turkeys. Every single one armed and aggressive and up for it. Joshing my little girl real crude, they were. And threatening the pump guy. We ain't used to it: this's just a call-in diner and gas station. No, Sheriff… *Muffleton Bottoms.* Not Mifflingtown Junction. Said they were taking these Hick and Back roads so they don't get your aitch-dubya patrols bugging them. Hick and Back, indeed. "Jes having a bit o' fun on the way to Philly," they said.

Time: 626 jikan: Zyhh to OS.2. Zyhh to OS.2. 'During the skirmish with Kumo forces we sustained a severe burnout of our central control bank. Succeeded in landing on an isolated humanic-type planet which appears to have an abundance of replacement parts. In particular, I have located a suitable, compact group that already has some unison of coordinated activity. All group members are aggressive, fast, and not excessively intelligent. Ten of them. They have adequate brain capacity; moderate observation skills and coordination. Could be ideal for our purposes. With your permission to go ahead, and use them as substitute units? Yes? Thank you. Yes, I have already detained them when they left the location of a personal and vehicular refuelling depot. No, their detention was not observed by others of their species. All being well, I can do that many extractions, one at a time. It'll simply take a little longer than usual to do clean removals working on my own. So, with your permission, OS.2, I shall perform the procedure immediately, and fit them into the banks one by one, instead of all ten in series at once. Can't afford to make cross-wiring mistakes like Jayeff Tee did last year, eh? Prelim tests indicate they should be readily controllable through pain administration, once they're fully interlinked in the system: they'll merely be an organic brain unit. With their aggression indices, we should be fine back in the combat orbits, far side of Sigmund. There is power available on this site as well, so I'll take the opportunity to re-charge the cells. Yes, back in action within about one jikan. Signing off – Zyhh.'

Time: 2100 hours: CNV-TS News. 'We are receiving reports of a particularly gruesome find in Central Pennsylvania, on the banks of the Juanita River. Staff and customers at the Muffins Diner and Gas Station have confirmed that ten bodies have been recovered from the vicinity. They are all adult males, and were discovered at a nearby scene where an area of woodland approximately two hundred feet diameter is reported to be completely flattened as though by a tremendous weight being placed there for some time. Many trees are crushed flat. A series of electric power lines has also been brought down and part-melted in the close vicinity, possibly by a lightning strike of immense power. Amateur cellphone footage appears to indicate that the ten bodies are naked and have had the contents of their heads removed. The County Coroner unofficially described the injuries as "brain-ectomies". In further communication, he said, "and, seemingly, their spinal cords have also been extracted. The whole of the Central Nervous System is missing. This has apparently been carried out with considerable technical skill." Initial on-site identification suggests that the bodies are those of a group of Pittsburgh Militia who had been travelling the backwoods route to Philadelphia to attend a rally in support of Gun Law Senator Pinkie Peewee. Final confirmation of all identities may take some time, the Knowall County Sheriff says.

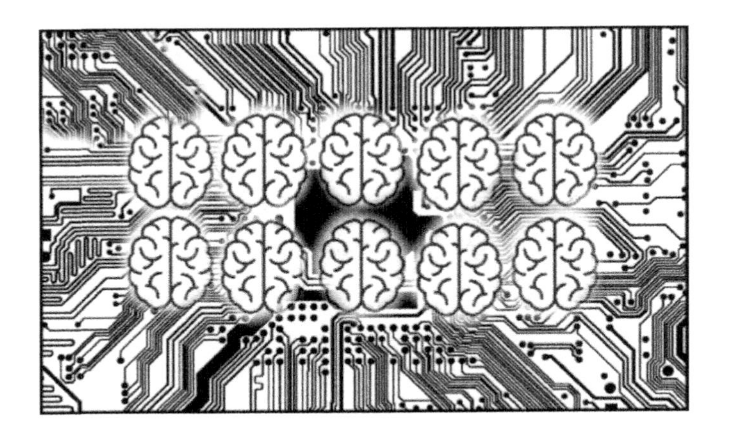

JEANNIE

'You're a weird one,' I told the picture of a golden-threaded rock on the laptop screen. 'I never noticed you on the dealer's table. *Are* you a face?' I twisted my head round. Then the screen. Puzzling and peering. 'You look a bit like a face from *this* angle. But from that angle, you're not. And from *here*, you're a definite maybe. Couple of blobs that could be like eyes, I suppose.'

I put the computer down, and picked up the beer can, trying to recall whether or not I'd studied that specimen individually when I bought it.

No, I don't think I did. For four days, I'd been traipsing round the Great Arizona Rocks, Gems and Fossils Show in Tucson, and I'd studied hundreds of rock and mineral specimens. Bought a couple of hundred so far, for the business. This morning an Australian dealer's stall drew me in. This guy was almost sold out of his native Australian minerals, so he was selling off the rest in job lots at a third of the first-asked price. It was so he could get a cheap flight home tomorrow, not wait round paying stall and room rent for five more days.

'I must have glanced at you,' I told the screen, 'cos I took the pic.' But, actually, I don't look when I do that: one hand dragging them across the table – stop; position; click; push aside. Who looks at what they're photographing? It's purely a matter of getting the focus and the framing right.

Anyway, the pics are just for the record – to remind me over the next six days what I've bought, so I don't buy repeats; to group them by mineral types; to decide which few I'd carry home to the U.K. and which I'd have shipped back. I'd put the best one on my web site tonight, with prices about ten times higher than I'd paid. Naturally – my flights, time, expenses, etc. needed to be covered. So I intended to spend a relaxing evening in my motel room with beer and whiskey, looking through the on-screen photographs of my latest purchases.

In truth, I just love them, every one. From amazonite to zircon, I drool over them. I've been known to vacantly stroke polished faces of minerals, or crystal facets when the cat isn't talking to me.

Mmm, I do remember this one. I'd moved it round a couple of times to get the light right, cleaned it with a quick spit and polish. It was a lump of tiger-eye; one of two dozen that were polished on one face, to reveal the golden silk-like fibres that seemed to be visible deep inside the rock.

I clicked through the next few photos… But that one intrigued me, so I clicked back to it. 'You could look like a face, I suppose. I must have a proper look at the real you when Ozzie brings the crate round later.'

'Fussy about them, eh?' The dealer had laughed. But they were his job lot. His choice, in effect, so I also wanted the photos to be sure he didn't substitute some before he brought them round to my motel after closing.

Yes, it had been a very good fair so far – I'd spent thousands on sunstones, opals, agates, selenites and the whole gamut of gorgeous minerals, stocking up for the year to come.

*

It's not that I forgot about the lump of rock with the slightly facelike swirl in it. It's simply that I'm a mug for supping my drink on warm evenings, the balmy scent of bougainvillea, sitting out on a motel veranda. So I'm afraid that won the day.

Thus, it was twenty-four hours later that I went through the Aussie's crate. 'Let's have a proper look at you, eh?'

It took ten minutes to find it, and I rotated the foot-long by five inches high piece of heavy rock – it has a high percentage of iron in it, that's what makes it so heavy. Between the mass of golden tiger-eye needles and the near-black base material it had an irregular triangular patch, three or four centimetres along each side, where there had been a gas bubble when the rock had been fluid and forming. Later, the bubble must have filled with the hot mineral fluids that kept seeping through the rock over the later ages; and it had created a swirl as it hardened.

Yes, the solidified eddy of mineral did look a bit like a face. Two patches could be imagined as eyes, but distortedly trapped within the rock. 'Well,' I laughed, a little the worse for the whisky, 'you can't have been in there all that time, not since the rock was formed; you're not two billion years old – the planet only had algae back then.

'Mind you, I must have been sloshed when I took this pic – you don't look quite the same now. 'But,' I checked where I'd put the bottle, 'that's enough time on you tonight, Jeannie.' I named her after a former lady-friend who had dark little eyes. 'There's all today's stuff to organise, and I can't afford to slip behind, or I'd never catch up.'

*

The following day was just as busy: buying, making new contacts, meeting a couple of customers. And a get-together in the evening with a few U.K. dealers I know. So I didn't have chance to look at any rocks or pics, much less have another look at that piece of tiger-eye.

*

I hadn't forgotten about her, but these are buying trips, not holidays, or *vacations*, as I keep hearing. So the day after that, I had to keep focused on the job and didn't have chance until late on, just before turning in. I'd propped the specimen up on the bedside table, 'You're different again, aren't you?' I turned the rock this way and that.

Then I realised what was happening. 'The fluid inside hasn't quite hardened. It's still shifting slightly, with the movement, and the warmth of the room and being handled. 'But,' I blearily studied the rock, 'you look a bit more like a face than you did two days ago.'

I turned it over again, suddenly imagining that I'd be making her dizzy. 'And you look worried.' Which only proves what a drunken nerdy fool I am, personifying an aberration in a lump of chalcedony fibres. I was thinking of a piece of rock as "she". But then, I often indulge in jokey-talking with superb specimens when I'm on solo buying trips, like, 'Who's gonna pay three grand for a smart piece like you, eh?' That was my chat-up line for an emerald crystal I'd seen.

But I was giving *her* an identity.

It, I mean.

*

Thursday evening, I went to the Longhorn Steakhouse on West Wetmore with some folks I met. They were Canadian and American dealers and miners. Nice folk and valuable buying contacts. Good night it was, too; very lively. So there wasn't much time for Jeannie.

But, traditional whiskey nightcap, sitting up in bed, I looked at her, sitting there next to the alarm clock. Yessss… the fluid inside that rock bubble had again shifted slightly. The eyes were better aligned as a pair, the mouth blob was small, like she was going, 'Oooh'.

I let her sit there. She could watch out for me overnight.

*

Busy all day, after a late start trying to keep up with the cataloguing and website specimens, so there wasn't much time that evening, either. Until the usual getting-into-bed time. 'Lord! Your eyes look too real. Your mouth's not right, though.' I had to laugh at myself and the wwhiskey glass, acting as if there was a miniscule someone trapped inside. A small part of someone, anyway – some of the head. 'Like her spirit,' I imagined. 'I should free you.'

But, a sanity-saving sip of San Miguel later, combined with further study, 'Don't be ridiculous,' I told her and Jack Daniels. 'You're merely a temporary chance growth of some treacly mineral resin. Although, this kind of rock used to be called "The Charms of Light." A beautifully appropriate name in your case, my dear.' So I drank to that.

*

It almost took courage to pick her up again on Saturday, and stroke over the smooth surface where the face was buried, wiping it as if to see more clearly, staring at the thumbnail-sized visage. The mouth wasn't forming right – some pin-head beads of crystal were spreading across the bubble, where her lower face should have been.

But your eyes – it's really bizarre how lifelike they look, Jeannie.' She was staring back at me! We made eye contact, dark eyes appealing to me for help. 'That's impossible.' But there's no mistaking it when you *do* make eye contact, even if only for a fraction of a second, and the head is scarcely an inch across.

I swallowed, nervous. It was idiotic. I argued with myself, 'Sure… right… who gets caught inside a block of stone?'

The obvious, definite answer came straight to me: A genie.

'Don't be stupid,' I told myself.

'Must be, though.' My imagination was running away with me. 'But what sort of genie are you?' I addressed the gleaming piece of polished stone, and promptly looked up everything about genies. Well, half a dozen sources on Google, anyway.

'Okay.' I eventually gazed at her again, having discovered that genies come in two very distinct types. Some even mated with people, according to Google. That'd be okay – she was a smart looker. Bit small, maybe. Like some folk reckon Adam and Eve were man and djinn… genie. 'So which are you? The guardian angel type who keeps watch over people in benevolent ways; the creative and friendly type who imparts wisdom? I could do with some of that, too.

'Or… are you one of those supernatural demon-genies created from the scorch of fire and wind? The ones who haunt people and buildings – and golden polished stones?'

Whether good spirits or evil demons, they aren't all great wispy hairy monsters, it seems: they come in all sizes and shapes, including just pieces of them, like heads or tails. Women as well as men.

'So a woman's head could well be a genie's spirit.' I scrutinised her tiny face – or actually, the lower face was gone now, the mineral beads drifting across it – almost like a veil. 'Yesss, Jeannie, you might be one. But I bet genies didn't get trapped in bottles and lamps and places for no reason – they'll have been wandering round causing mayhem, mischief and trickery, pushing things too far. 'Is that the sort you are? A bucket of trouble? Is that what happened?'

I laughed, turning the smooth stone over in my hands for the umpteenth time, wondering if someone at the quarry where it was found had polished this piece of rock down to this surface by design or chance. Stopped short in fear? Or never even noticed, if the triangle bubble had only been a smeary swirl?

Stroking over the glassy surface, a couple of millimetres from her cheek, I wondered, not for the first time, whether or not I should release her. If so, how? 'Come on. Don't be stupid. It's a lump of tiger-eye rock.'

But the eyes looked so real, whichever way I turned the rock. And it was definitely like a veil below the eyes now. Suppose she really was real? And the wayward sort? Could I take any precautions? Yes, I should shut the door to keep her in. Yes, right – the massive towering evil hulk that sweet-faced little Jeannie would morph into was going to be constrained by a closed motel room door. Sure it would. Also… also… I shouldn't chisel at the rock too hard in case it gave her a headache and she got mad at me. She would have to wait: I had work to do. But… I stopped. If I kept her waiting, she might get mad about that, too. Wasn't Sinbad's genie angry about being kept waiting for thousands of years?

Too wrought up over the whole silly mess, I was actually trembling. I was going to do it: smash a fifty-quid piece of rock apart because I'd talked myself into it over a few days working and heavy drinking.

But I *couldn't* leave somebody locked up in there forever. Oh, Lord. I've just *got* to.

Ready…

It's a pity I can't keep my fingers crossed when I'm holding a cold chisel in one hand and a lump hammer in the other. 'I bet you haven't been to England before, have you, Jeannie? You'll like it.' I patted the rock reassuringly, positioned the chisel, and raised the hammer…

She's looking so hopeful in there…

Steady…

Wow...

KJID

'There's a human coming! Here. To Middore. There's a crowd of us going down to see. Supposed to be dropping down from Orbit One. Yoogs! *A human!*'

'I just been hearing on the pods – Seems like it came into orbit over the last two days, decelerating. Staticked over Tinn Town at dawn today.'

Three of Tosis's antenna swivelled to the unrevealing sky as though in search of the humanic spacecraft somewhere directly above.

There *must* have been some kind of contact by the gov. Yoogs, *a human!* Here of all places.'

'Yeah, right. So it's a human. So what we done wrong, then?'

'Or right. Could be some perfectly valid reason.'

'Or something totally incomprehensible.'

'Yeah, what? Like borrow a cup of T Lenium?'

Mixima's anal frills gyrated in giggles at the thought of a fabled human popping round for a T-Len fuel cell replenishment.

'They just been on about it on the TriVees and the pods – like it's some First Time Ambassador from Humanic Fed is coming in.'

'Does gov know why it's here?'

'Nothing official been said, as far as I can glean.'

'You think they're subsuming us into the 'Manic Fed… their Empire?'

Tosis spectrumed through the colour charts at the prospect of being ruled, dominated by aliens… *humans.* 'OmiClod,' he said.

‘Well, they’re sure not here to surrender, are they? Fed as powerful as the Humanic?’

‘Surrender? We’re not at war with’em, are we?’

‘Don’t think so. But you never know.’

‘I heard about what they did on Croyde—'

‘Yoogs, yes – the locals didn’t stand a chance, poor little yoogers.’

‘And it’s said there was only a few of’em, on a planet the size and power of Croyde.’

‘They tried to reckon afterwards it was just a fleet of competitors and supporters for the shuttlecraft bow-surfing championships – but they veered off-course when one-of-em’s engine de-phased, and they thought they might as well run their own games in the thicker atmosphere there.’

Mixima curdled his proboscal juices as he considered the utter madness of bow-surfing a shuttle down from orbit. *Humans, huh?*

‘Are you coming down to see? Momentous event.’

‘Well, I never seen one before…’

‘Ain’t many of us has. Come on, then. Now’s your chance to have a gander.’

‘What? Down the ’Port? And stand there with all the long-neckers tri-balling some… some… invader – cos that’s what it is, you know. They get a tentacle-tip in somewhere and there’s no getting rid of them.’

Tosis’s carapace vibrated in delicious horror to imagine the terror of it all, especially if the human got at Racnid first and knotted a few antennae.

‘Here, look. That’s its ship now. Just a lander, must have a tight-packed landing party in there.’

'No – the word I'm getting down the pods is that it's only one human unit coming to the surface.'

'And up there? Massed electro-power ranged in on us, they think?'

'They haven't said. Implicit threat, I expect. The hard and silent treatment. Keep us on our tarsals.'

'No word about any messages, then? No hints? What is it, Battleweight Niner?'

'They an't said – top secret, I expect. Don't want to curl our anal frills, do we? let'em know about our capability?'

'Indeed not,' Mixima and Tosis entwined antennae in mutual mental union as the unsettling idea of curled anal frills came to them.

'I can't stand the waiting much longer, Mix. Wait. Look at the hull… there's a crack. Circular… it's an opening in the side.'

'I can see movement. It's going to appear. It'll come out. Maybe…'

'Twine my tentacles, Mix. I'm feeling weak at the frills. It'll—'

'There… look… it's coming out…'

'Urr, *little* innit?'

'Don't look much…'

'I've had bigger breakfasts…'

'You could snap that in half.'

'Bet that top lump'd come off dead easy.'

'I think that's their nerve centre – all the vocals, visuals… All its processing oddments stored in that bit.'

Antennae aquiver, Mixima took in the planet-changing event – *first contact!* – a visit by a human.

'What sort is it?'

'Sorts? What? They come in different types?'

'I know they have two kinds. They're called male and female.'

'What for?'

'How would I know? Social standing? Master and slave? Reproduction? Yes, that's it, I think I heard – It takes two, they say.'

'Wonder what this one is?'

'No idea. Maybe the differences aren't visible, or too insignificant to the untrained eye to tell. P'raps not important to them.'

Tosis's thoracic plates crinkled to think of body-form variations – Appalling concept – the End of Conformity as we know it.

Crowding closer... 'This is *First Contact.*' The whisper was going round. 'History in the making.'

'Look, look. That's a step-ramp unfurling. Right down to the ground.'

'Everyone, back.' The horde of onlookers bristled into reverse.

'It moved! Look! OmiClod! It has leg-things.'

'Looks precarious on them – there's only two to balance on.'

'It's coming down... *Back... back...*'

Tosis fibrillated in near-panic as the creature began the descent.

'Hope it stops there. Is that a weapon it's carrying? An explosives container?'

'Maybe a translator?'

'Must be someone here who speaks Humanic...?'

'What for? Never been any need.'

'Listen, it's making sounds...'

Its top lump moved in all directions, as if it was looking around.

"Kjid."

Every antenna in the crowd picked up the First Word Ever by a human on the planet. It carried on making the sounds... '*Niww eunxk. Llwwd; I u3r6293e800101001; ??? Kp qoesx smdvnd fqwjskd wed jnc; Oak k wj qkdf powjo jj okdjf..."*

Open-mandibled, Tosis heard it pronounce all the tinkling, jarring vibrations, and watched it turn around several times. 'Yoogs, Mixima, that is so frightening. Those eye-sensors... seeing everywhere. Did you catch any of what it said?'

'Not a tone. I think the noise came out that variable hole at bottom centre of the top-lump.'

'I can feel those vision sensors eating into me.' Mixima's nerve control was nearing overload.

'Ah... just a min... I'm getting a pod saying it stores all its monitoring equipment and controls in that top lump – the central processing area, all the vision, smell, gustation, balance, acceleration, auditory, propriocentricity, time, thermal...'

'Yes, yes, I get the idea. We're dead if it turns on us.'

'I feel weak,' Tosis wailed through three sets of mandibles. 'Look at it.'

'Might be little, but it's the creature from The Pit.'

'There's such threat in that voice. All the complexity of things on top – that mass of fine frills hanging down from the very top. And those visual sensors – eyes – they're sort of glittering at us.'

'I think I just dried myself,' Mixima confessed in shame.

‘There’s another ’cast coming down the pods – they’re working on the translation of what it said.’

‘Back, back. It’s moving, coming among us. I can’t move, my bristles have frozen.’ *A Human.*

Mixima knew his spiracles had expanded to take in more of the same air that the human was in- and exhaling. ‘To breathe the same air… be in the presence of such… awesomeness…’

‘OmiClod, it’s coming this way, to us.’

‘Ohhhh…’

‘Ooooh…’

‘I can’t move.’ Tosis wailed again.

‘Podcast thinks they can do a near-simultaneous translation if it makes more sounds…’

It stood before them, as they cowered lower. It seemed to tower over them now they were sinking low. So overwhelming. A side appendage reached into the container it was carrying. The human emitted sounds once more. To the auditory sensor-membranes of Mixima and Tosis they sounded the same as previously. Completely unintelligible.

‘There’s a tentative translation coming through the pods,’ Mixima whispered. ‘I think it must be in some kind of code…’

‘Hello.

‘I’m everso lost. Silly me. Women pilots, eh? I thought I’d dobbed the right coordinates in the Navi-panel… See? I have the right figures right here in my bag. I thought I was a long time getting here. Do you know where these coordinates would be? I’m supposed to be shopping on Planet Vuitton.’

KYRE?

Stabbing pain. Awareness from nothing in an instant.

Gasping to breathe. Mouth and nose blocked with slime. Eyes, too. Can't breathe… or scream. Choking, drowning in heavy gripping mud.

I'm sinking; trying to scream. Something foul writhing in my throat. Gagging, clutching for it. Fingers can't reach it. Retching on the taste... the stench. Sinking more. Struggling… so weak.

Exhausted. Can't carry on. Making it worse. Collapsing back. Need to stop – wait. Rest, not fight. Must stop – not sink further. Wait… *'Kyre hresh...?* What's happened? Where am I?'

Wait… wait. Let the pain ease… strength return. Crawling things against my skin. Near-buried in mud. Wait… wait…

**

Shuddering with cold; scarce breathing. I'm in a world of glooping mud. And zipping shrill insects. 'Who am I? *Ky-toin?'* What the *fryke* has happened to me?'

A single weak, choking cough. Not enough to rid myself of a finger-pinch of filth, never mind the thing that still squirms in my throat. Confused whirling in my head… What am I? I have a mouth? Hands? Face? Is this pain I feel? I don't know of pain, yet I feel as much pain as there is mud.

Think back; can only be a few moments ago. I *must* know who I am… what I am. What is this place? Where am I?

Why am I here?

Wait… wait…

**

'Gerrimahterthere!'

'Gerrold ovim!'

'Stop struggling y' cunny.'

Voices! Loud and close. Raucous. Crashing into my head. Splitting my mind. 'Wha's app…?'

Grasped and heaved, being dragged through mud, branches and leaves. *Kuit!* – my naked body, trailing legs, slimed and bloodied. Struggling, I'm dragged out the mud… dumped onto a rotting log.

This is me? This convulsing body? What am I? Can't stop the shudders. Blood pouring down my chest and my arm. Can't cough… scarce breathe. Men hitting my back. Shouting, laughing. So loud. Black mud spurting out my mouth; blood splattering down me. *Kuit!* My side's split open in a huge rip, flesh straining out, blood pouring, mud-worm squirming, sinking back within.

Panic fading. Gasp a breath. Look round at hard faces and drawn swords. Men in muddied, dull-green uniforms. This is all so wrong. The whole stinking place reeking of decay. 'You're soldiers? Who are you? You *odiousi* creatures?'

In some awful guttural language, they demand and sneer; laugh and poke at me, asking something, pointing up into the trees, at broken branches. Huge splatters of mud adorning drapes of grey lichen.

'Me? I fell? Through the trees?' Can't shake the dullness away. 'Where the *kuit* from?'

**

A pair of troopers closed round me, peering and prodding at my head, muttering. 'What's wrong up there? *Kyre rej?'* I asked. No answer. I reached up, *'Fryke!'* A jagged split.

One of them, a scar across his face, grunted, and jerked my hand away, and splashed swampy water over my head. He picked, teasing fragments away, showing me splinters of bone. And wood. I *had* fallen through the trees. Our eyes met. We both grimaced.

'*Yye froik.* That doesn't look good.' I stared disbelievingly at the bone fragments. My head's shattered? I was finished before I started. Started what? *Why am I here?*

Some of the men jabbered, pointing at my eyes.

'My eyes? What about them? *Gahi Kyre?'*

One forced into my mouth, fingers clawing, tugging out a flat-headed worm. Another prised two more from my skin. Vile things. Poking, digging into my side, deep inside, working another writhing creature from within.

Forced the pain to wash away… *'Na Kyre?* What do you want? Who are you?'

No-one answered. A baffled shrug. More incomprehensible muttering and head-shaking. One raised a sword over me. Scarface pushed it away, rapping orders. A rope slipped round my neck. I grabbed at it, *'Kyre hruuki…?* What are you doing?'

Too late. No strength. Dragged upright, swaying. Tried to resist, but I was forced away with a sword thrust and jerk on the neck rope. So that's where I'd been – in a splatter-pit, a crater of mud. Filthy brown-green water oozing back into it.

**

The faint, twisting trail was a torment, staggering through sucking mud and ensnaring vines, compelling me to keep going with incessant curses, sword stabs and jerks on my neck tether. Equally vicious little creatures snapped at my ankles, and swarms of insects plagued everywhere I bled – and that seemed to be everywhere.

‘Hateful *maluki: that* one – called Scoppo – just loves using his sword. And *that* one who laughs so much. *Him*, jerking the rope. Not one of them understands a word I speak. *Voitugs!* They die.’

**

‘Grallator! Grallator!’ Yelling, the troopers scattered into the swamp. I was alone. Mud-caked and naked. My tether hung free. Nowhere to go.

A dozen paces ahead: a crouched creature, covered in armoured scales, with a mouth to chew a man in half. Legs widespread, straddling the way, swaying slightly. My heart drooped into the mud with the troopers. ‘So, you’re a grallator, hmm?’

A whipping, barbed tail twanged like a straightening spring. I dipped; a trilth of a beat before it zizzed through the air where my neck had been. *Fryke!* It was fast. I crouched lower, trembling, and watched it bite down at a uniformed corpse, now headless. It growled, raising its head, as though fixing on me. Double rows of yellow-brown teeth, a killing system, backed up by a mass of writhing worm-like tongues. It glowered back across the trampled trail between us. Its tail lashed again, mouth opening in a silent roar, shoulders tensing, readying to come at me.

‘You want me, do you? Not if—' I threw myself at it, half-rolling, grabbing a fallen wayside branch. Off-balance, the branch out in front of me, hurling myself at the beast.

So *fast* – hardly aware of my own movements, ramming the splintered end into the open mouth, deeper and deeper. Ranting at the monstrous *retilja,* forcing the branch inwards with all my weight and remaining strength. *Kuit!* I was shot through in searing pangs.

It bellowed and flailed, the hot stench of rotted stomach breath buried me, dagger-teeth snapping into the branch, raking along my arm. *'Ky-yack!!* – my hand!' Deep score-marks spurted blood.

Half leaping, half-thrown by a swing of its thrashing head, I was spinning over backwards. Scrambling away, hardly aware of what I was doing. Beyond the range of the frenziedly-lashing tail, I knelt low, reaching to a second part-buried branch. *Careful... fingers grasping.* Crouched, watching the grallator as it raged, head waving wildly; long, taloned legs clawing at the protruding branch in its jaws, until it fell free, heavily bloodied. A moment more of fury and tail-whipping, a final, blood-spraying bellow, and it stamped howling into the swamp, raising clouds of insects and noxious vapours.

'Skoig oiff!' I cursed as it vanished.

I sagged. 'Where the *Jebem* did speed like that come from? In me? *Kuit!* I was fast.' And shocked at my own sheer violence.

Still on my knees, absolutely exhausted. The pain, effort, lost blood. Barely aware of the drab uniforms floundering back from the quagmire and root entanglements. Shaking, I breathed again, but couldn't even attempt to stop one of the troopers retrieving the neck tether, and adding a second one.

'Kyre vai? What am I?'

They pushed the mangled body of their former comrade aside. Dragged to my feet, the trek restarted.

'Yordy,' Scarface said, as we trooped past the abandoned remains, dark blood seeping into the sucking ooze – the first wriggles of hidden creatures already homing in.

'Kyre yu? These *vaahtos* left me here to join you, eh, Yordy?'

I detested them. Scarface was probably the only one who was not swamp-born scum. Our eyes met again, for a beat. Perhaps fellow-feeling, before the rope jerked, and I was dragged onward.

'Shu gustya.' I spat a mouthful of gunge and blood at the trooper gripping the rope, and bared my teeth at the one who held the new tether behind me. Both men flinched. That was better – my victory; my first smile.

**

A more urgent pace. The mass of gashes and grazes brought more pain. Ducking under low-hanging branches, constantly tripping over tangles of roots, I staggered through the mud and clutching vines. Unending, foul-tempered yanks at the neck leashes forced me on; plus the hilarious jabs from Scoppo's delightful sword. More and more, my hate concentrated on the ugly-grinning little *voitug*. 'Just give me one chance, you *vaahto.'*

He grinned, full of confidence. Swung his vicious blade…

**

A piercing two-note sound stopped us. The troopers listened and conferred – *that* direction. The brutal speed picked up again. A two-beat pause when the peal of notes sounded again, closer. Feet stumbled around the umpteenth chaos of creepers and hanging mosses, the ground seemed firmer, drier.

A clearing… Ahead, a high tower loomed, rising from a timber and wicker stockade wall. The troopers' shouts were answered by sentinels atop the tower.

My neck jerked forward; Scoppo grinned.

'You die. Definite. *Voitug*.' I snarl-smiled at him.

Another wrench. Another curse. Heavy wooden gates swung menacingly open.

‘Need to get my head clear… gain strength.’ I didn’t know who I was appealing to, but I really needed help from somewhere.

**

The gates closed behind us, seeming to seal my fate. The air seemed suddenly darker in the settling gloom of evening, as heavy beams dropped into place. Hauled across a bare clearing, into the clamorous, stinking disorder of an army camp. All around were troopers and animals, smoking fires and fluttering banners, high tents and sheaves of stacked pikestaffs.

Taller than all others, I stared over the throng of drab uniforms and eager faces that crowded around us. A confusion of demanding, scowling troopers, egged on by the jeering Scoppo.

The evil little *vaahto* poked at the gaping split in my side; pointed at my eyes, between my legs, and the wide-open head wound. They seemed to be jabbering about every part of me, as I swayed in their midst. Yordy was mentioned, the men imitating the swing of the grallator’s tail, pointing at me.

Dulled by the numbing pain, legs buckling, I mumbled, *‘Kyre shoit?* Who are you rabble? Leave me be – I need to think. Need to remember.’

A broad, dark-uniformed trooper, three silver stripes on each shoulder, pushed through. The others made way for him – a man of some rank, if not height. Glaring red-faced up at me, his rasping, spittle-flecked interrogation meant nothing. They were all increasingly angry, shouting and arguing, until something was suddenly decided. They shrugged, waved at me dismissively.

‘Hric cui…? No further interest to you, am I?’ That much was obvious. I wasn’t sure if that was a relief. Or more ominous.

**

In a beat, I was stumbling away – pushed and dragged through the horde, to a stake where a dozen coarse-haired animals rose, growling as we approached, needle fangs bared, back hair erect. One of the troopers said something about *hounds*, forcing me to the ground. He knotted the rope to the same post as the animals. Laughing, he kicked at me, swaggered away.

After the horrendous slog and stink through the swamp, the rich warmth of animal reek was almost comforting. Naked and shuddering, I sagged, befuddled. I don't think I ever felt that way before. It was… what? Humiliation. I didn't like it.

'*Kyryck…? So, Fanged Ones, w*hat do I do when you attack, hmm?'

But, as the moments crept by, and they didn't move, I began to believe they weren't going to attack, and I didn't feel so afeared, nor as shudderingly shocked by the whole thing. 'You're accepting me, are you?' I reached to the nearest one, let it smell my hand. Briefly, it licked at the blood. Strange – it didn't worry me – I wasn't getting any feel of death-lust from them. 'You'll share your warmth, eh?'

Couldn't think – a swirling red mist covered everything. But I had to sort through my mind – the tangling thoughts – think back. *'Kyre reck?'* I appealed to the hounds. 'Who am I? What is this body I have? It's damaged. Badly? And who are these *vaahto*-men yelling at me like *skacks* on heat? If that sadistic little Scoppo *fryker* sticks me once more…'

I raked into the fur of the closest hound. '*Kimji Kyre voi?* Do you know what they're planning, eh?' The teeth-baring beast answered with a low growl. I growled back. *'Mie ti…* Come closer, Warm One.' I pulled at it, feeling it resist a moment before shuffling beside me and accepting my arm around it. It didn't growl any more. I felt better.

The gloom deepened, and I sniffed a rich aroma of spiced food from the camp fires. Another of the hounds came snuffling uncomfortably close to my groin. '*Jresh...?* Getting restless? We're all in the same *javola,* are we?'

Slumped against the post, I waited, and the minins stretched. Tried to relax my tensed-up muscles, and slow down my spinning mind. *Who am I? What am I?* Two dozen paces away, the flame-silhouetted mob of soldiery stamped round, stoking the fires up, voices raised in sudden laughter.

'Ahh, the drinks are out, hmm?' The hounds didn't answer. 'Well, whatever they plan for me, I'm more rested now; and I'm not shaking so much.'

'Come.' I dug my fingers into the neck fur of the beasts on either side of me. 'You'll share your strength with me, won't you, my *killi* friends? I suspect I may need it before long.'

**

The wait stretched gratefully out; the men were settling; more wood went on the fires; a group began chanting. Eventually, two gloating troopers headed my way, jabbering together as they towered over the hounds and me. I managed to smile back. 'You *voitugs* speak in the tongue of worms for all the sense you make. *Kyre inik?* My turn for dinner, is it?'

Twisting the tethers free, they hauled me up, and dragged me towards the main fire before I could get my balance. Staggering into the middle of a circle of baying soldiers, I stood alone, still the tallest there. They were readying themselves for something… something to do with me. Ritual execution, I imagined.

'So, I'm the *oyin kulji*, am I, the entertainment? One of these *vaahto* creatures is readying to attack, hmm? Which one?' Alert as a *goyat* mother, I studied them all, tried tensing and untensing my muscles: some felt unweakened. Others were gone. The stocky soldier with silver stripes stood slightly alone, prominent among them. They didn't like to crowd him too much, hmm? He would make a clear target, should I need to attack.

Take the advantage – with all the flamboyance I could muster, I spat at the nearest tormenter, flexed my fingers in anticipation of how I might retaliate when he launched at me. Perhaps, just perhaps, if that swamp-born speed comes to me again, I might survive longer. The trooper was considering his choices. Carefully, I coiled the tethers around one forearm. Swaying, stumbling without even moving, I tensed, ready to burst into movement when he – or another of them – pounced.

A shout! A commotion. Attention switched to two people pushing closer: both so different from the weather-beaten faces and forest-green-and-mud uniforms of the soldiery. One was a tall man in a dark uniform, gold braided. The other was small, in scarlet apparel with black cording, and a face that was smooth, with pale cheeks. I stared down as the smaller one came close. My mind blanked. *What are you?* Slender fingers reached to me. I flinched as they trailed across my body, where the open slash still trickled blood. *'Hruish?'* A strange shock as I realised, 'You're… *a woman?'*

Turning, she berated the troopers, ranted at Silver Stripes and argued with her companion; turning to prod at the blood-crusted split in my side, pointing up to my head, and the equal split up there. Angry, she demanded something of me. I had no idea what, and silently stared back. She renewed her argument with Gold-Braid, pushing the jeering troopers back, her arms waving more urgently. Silver Stripes argued with her and Gold-Braid; all asking and demanding; troopers gesturing skywards, arms dropping in a sudden fall, and great splatter.

'*Kyre ti?* That was me again, Hmm? Falling from the sky?'

Another decision. The woman raged at the two decision-makers, and fought against the muddy green uniforms who held her back. She didn't look too happy with me, either. 'Perhaps you're averse to blood-and-mud-cloaked monsters?' I wondered. 'You had your own plans for me, eh, woman?' But she hadn't had her way – the circle re-enlarged around me. Cheering and chanting, they were ready to continue.

Radiating confidence, it was sword-sticking Scoppo who stepped forward, twirling his blade with well-practiced ease, clearly expecting an easy and amusing triumph. A bragging jest, accompanied by deft whirling of the blade in the direction of my groin.

'Good of you to tell me what you intend, hmm?'

The troopers' impatient yells sparked in my head, added a sharper edge, and I sank into a defensive crouch. 'You gruesome little *voitug*. You mean to slice bits off me, hmm? *Nai mie.*'

I fixed a rock-smile on him… increasingly aware of the fire's heat; the tang of smoke and burned food; the uneven ground. Scoppo's teeth reflected the fire, red and ugly, bared in a confident snarl. The changing hand-grip; the light footwork, over-playing to his audience; stepping close, reaching down to me. Down… down… He was so *slow*…

So much time… In a dozenth of a heartbeat, I had him. Rigid fingers rammed straight through his eyes, destroying the arrogance. I clutched, cartwheeling over, ripping out the middle of his face; hurling him back. Staying on him, I crushed him down, smashed a fist into his throat. His neck bones crunching most satisfyingly.

I spat into the dead and ruined face, *'Visco, Shirick* – Riddance, Accursed One.' And tore the sword from his failed grasp. 'Remain calm; stay on the corpse. There'll be more. This sword hilt feels good.' I adjusted my grip, and spat defiant blood at the nearest troopers as they recommenced their chant, and clattered swords on their scabbards. Faces lit up from within as well as from the fire. *'Kyre rashi?* Who's next?'

A low growl behind me. Stupid to warn me. I dropped aside. Rolled to my feet. My newly-acquired sword lancing of its own accord. Straight through the gaping mouth of the trooper launching at me. I side-stepped. A wrist-flick, and his brains were stirred as he toppled face down into the fire.

'Not so entertained now, are you, *moi kytterlings?'* Inside, I shook, but found grim pleasure in disposing of two of my tormenters. I treated the rest to a challenging, bared-teeth snarl, and waited.

The mass of shouted advice from his encrowding supporters didn't make the next one any less careless, confident that I was tumbling off-balance. His face a sudden picture of disbelief as the steel blade sliced into his guts, and his bowels slurped, glistening, by the fire, as he descended slowly among them.

'Kyre ruti? Who now? Wait, wait,' I ordered myself. 'Wait, see.' Swaying badly, I could scarce stand. But needed to watch them. Which next?

They quietened in the flickering firelight. The sword was slipping from my grasp; fingers numbed. 'Strength, *Ti Kyre* – I need strength. Come to me.' The troopers edged, shuffling, undecided about their amusement now.

That *riuff* woman was still close by, still screeching and yappering her protests. Glancing, yes, *there*. Watching us. I stared back at them. 'Braided Uniform's annoyed – keeps shushing her. *Ti mie voi...?* You still want me, do you, woman? It'd stir you up if I could get to you, eh, *Uniform?* Ah, these two on my left – they've agreed their tactics? All their nodding and eye-flicking? Coming... *Now!'*

The instant they leapt forward, I side-stepped – no thought, no plan. As though of its own accord, my sword cleaved straight down through one trooper's head, splitting it in ghastly halves. I rammed his over-fleshy comrade backwards, crushing him flat on his back in a heartbeat. Tubby gasped something fear-filled, face a mask of amazed horror.

Silence shrouded them all... breath held. Blood dripped into Tubby's left eye from the point of the sword I had poised over him. He was down and out. I hesitated... '*Kyre huig?* You concede?' He wouldn't know the words, but he knew what I meant, alright. They all did.

A loud shout. Commanding. Braided Uniform was demanding something of the woman. She nodded repeatedly; eagerly. He hesitated... dismissed her to the shadows with a wave, and stepped forward.

'So you've agreed something with the woman, have you? *Druis yai?* What this time?' I kept the blade hovering over the fat one's face, splitting my attention between him, the advancing Uniform, and the edging-closer troopers.

'Captain,' Uniform said, patting his own chest, 'Captain Briand.' He was afraid. Of me. Visibly trembling, he gestured for me to surrender the sword.

'What do I do? *Ria voi?* I should trust *you?'*

Uniform – Captain – gestured again for the sword. What else to do? Attack them all? Carry on like this? Not realistic against all of them. Deeply untrusting, eyes wide, I started to rise.

A too-fast movement from Tubby. His blade sliced up. I twisted away, *'Kaka!* Fool!' He died instantly, Scoppo's sword slamming through his right eye, spiking his head tight to the ground. 'You treacherous *bakho* creature.'

He'd slit me across my belly. A stinging, biting pain and yet more blood. How could I trust them? The sword sucked out Tubby's eye socket, and I raised it slowly, to within a hand's width of Uniform's belly. He stood his ground, shaking more than I was. *'Soiking Vaahto.* You're fearful, aren't you?' It was almost amusing. He barked orders to the soldiery, waved them back, and stretched out a hand to me for the sword, speaking again in quiet tones.

'The entertainment's off, is it, *mi kuik?* Trying to reassure me?' The same debate inside. What do I do? Attack them all? *Frykit!* I had to risk him again… lowered the sword a second time. *'Kyre rashi?* You know you're dead if that happens again, Uniform… Captain? *Tio Theron.'*

'Kyre?' The captain repeated it, and beckoned Silver-Stripes forward, rapping orders to him. Both said Kyre several times. They knew not what it meant. I told them, but they had no understanding. Pointing at me, as though calling me Kyre. Then telling me the broad silver-stripe one was called Mink. '*Bannerman* Mink.' Patting his own chest again. '*Captain* Briand.'

I tried to stand. Couldn't. Raised the sagging sword again. *'Nai Kyre...* Kyre's not my name. It means Question – I ask a question.'

But it was obvious Captain and Silver-Stripe Mink didn't understand. They repeated it. 'Kyre,' pointing at me, 'Kyre.'

'So, I'm called Question, am I?' I tried to think, 'I'm not Kyre. I'm... I'm... *Thron? Theron?*' But my thoughts were fading, joining my memories in the blankness. I had no idea who I was.

Ky-oh, what to do? Accept it? I half-nodded to them, knowing I couldn't keep the sword – they'd attack me, all at once, if I refused to give it up. *'Kiri hagg.'* In a last burst of defiance, I thrust the long blade into the fat one's rounded chest and rammed it home. It had a gratifying effect on the surrounding troopers, as they all seemed to shrink back a fraction, affording me the opportunity to slip Tubby's dagger inside the wrapping of corded tethers around my forearm.

Standing next to the two Uniforms, I gave the assembled soldiery a long stare, and growled like a hound. I know it was stupid, but they got the idea. And it raised a smile for me while I wondered what was next to come: 'I've killed five troopers at what should have been my execution. What now? Back with the hounds, am I? While these two consider more entertaining ways to kill me? That woman, too – where's she gone? *Troi gasri?* Given up, has she? Or up to some malign scheme of her own?'

It was comforting to feel the dagger's hilt, buried in the coiled tether. I turned to the higher uniforms without one iota of trust. I tried to keep what tiny advantage I had, and summoned up enough arrogance to deliberately irritate them. Straightening, looking down on them all, I sneered around, waved them to lead the way, to whatever they had in mind for me. *'Hoi! Vaahtos...'*

**

They escorted me through the mob of gawping troopers, the captain rapping out his orders again; the bannerman arguing. A small enclosure with high wicker walls was what they had in mind. Large animals were tethered to rails outside.

The two uniforms continued to argue: Silver Stripes demanding and loud; the captain calm and insistent. I watched, 'You want different things of me, hmm? One wants me dead; the other has plans for me... and the woman? I expect you'll take turns with your own schemes.'

Pushed into a dimly-lit compound, a motion across the throat conveyed the idea that I shouldn't attempt to leave. Behind me, bolts grated into place, and the arguing continued: they seemed to have a fondness for bolts and arguments. I stared into the dung-reeking darkness, nervous of what might be there, but feeling slightly more secure with the dagger clutched tight. *'Kyrith ki?* So what's in this place?' Movement. Four men were sitting together in the near-black corner, staring my way. A couple of water pails by my feet. A heap of loose pelts and blankets filled the opposite corner. 'They'll do. At least I get a rest.'

I stumbled across, and reached down to the furs. *Fryke!* Pain bit through me! Plus the powerful stink of wet fur, on top of my own swamp and blood stench. The mound moved. *'Toi gaic* – someone's in there already. Damn!' I sank to the ground next to the heap, readjusting my grip on the knife, and leaning back against the heavy wickerwork. 'I need to retch. Did I swallow some of those vile worms? Or just mud? What the *kroit* is happening? *Kyre moi?* Who am I?' I shivered, chilled by the cooling air, the slaughter of five men, the incubus trek to this ghastly place, and desperate to know who the *fryke* I was.

Very tentatively, I touched at patches of numbness, areas that oozed and ached. *'Liru kyre?* Am I still alive?' I felt at the wounds across my head and side… my belly. 'Oh, *Kroitit* – Tubby's knife-slash's feels worse than I imagined. Be lucky to make it to first light – too much blood lost; too much mud and mould taken in. Then the noisome threesome'll be fighting over my scraps.' I almost managed to laugh at the prospect, 'Give me rest… some sustenance… and we'll see.'

A movement among the furs, *'Kyre ets?* Who's there?' Heavily shadowed eyes peered at me. 'I watched warily as a slender hand appeared. It beckoned. I hesitated only a beat, and shuffled sideways under the raised kurk. Grateful to whoever… whatever, I let the long coarse-haired pelts envelop me in warmth, half-expecting another knife in my stomach. *'Keetai,'* I muttered in thanks, gradually settling, with an awareness of welcome body warmth, less alone in the darkness.

A touch on my upper arm startled me. Smooth fingertips caressed my skin, exploring me. *'Jebem!* Why would…? The woman?' I checked the dagger again. 'I know nothing about such creatures. There's something worrying about them? They're an unknown peril? *Kroit!* Is she *that* woman?'

Fingers stroked… pressed delicately at my skin, paused at a crusted, bloody patch; then slithered onward. *'Hoi-tu!'* she triggered something in me. 'What does she intend? Is this some dreadful mistake? Dare I reach to her? Surely can't be worse than my experiences with men.'

'Yarrah!!!'

'Volgoy—' Shattering voice bursting above me. Two men. Wrenching at the furs that covered us. I raged upwards. Tubby's dagger slashed into one's face, tearing a great flap of flesh away before plunging to the hilt in his throat. The man had no lower-body clothing, something protruded like a baton. His partner was slow. The dagger tore him apart in five raging beats. Panting with tension, half-crouched, I took a final rent at each corpse, 'What now? Damn, it's all ended now.'

My furs-fellow strode across the open compound, bending briefly over the two survivors. A blade flashed momentarily. *'Shai chi!* She really is a *she* – the shape, the way she walks. Yesss... she's the captain's irritant. So what was it she wanted me for?'

Unspeaking, we struggled to heap all four corpses in their corner. She pulled at their clothing, gathering a selection of coats and trews, shirts and boots, and tossed them to the pile of furs we had just vacated.

Whatever she'd intended, my encounter with her was finished, wrecked by these *frykers* in the corner. For some reason, I was immensely disappointed, *'Fryke* them. Just when something was about to happen.' I wasn't sure what, but – *Svecki!* – it had felt good. Furious, I slashed at their faces, rage taking over from the memory of that warm-body near-experience. 'Though perhaps not completely,' as I looked down at my nakedness.

She was back beside me, dismissing the corpses with a curling lip and a shrug, 'Brigands... Bandits... *Come.*' The words sounded familiar. That's what Scarface, in the swamp patrol had said, and Silver Stripes.

Gesturing, she pulled me beneath the dim entrance lights. Pressed me onto an upturned wooden pail, and began to wash me, slowly and deliberately, using water from a second, leather pail. For an age I suffered the rubbing and poking, both of us grimacing as she pulled wood and bone splinters from the gashes in my head and side. I shuddered with the cold and unending pain, gritted my teeth, and forced myself not to jerk away from fingers that determinedly pried and picked and probed at me.

She turned to the long split across my stomach, where the fat little *fryker's* dagger had sliced. Holding up a bone needle and a length of thread, she asked something. I didn't understand, until she pulled the sides of the wound together, and forced the needle through the brought-together flesh. Screaming inside, I clamped my eyes shut, tight-balled my fists, and endured an eon of fiery agony as she crudely stitched across my stomach.

Sinkingly miserable and disappointed, I attempted to divert my thoughts from the injuries: *'Kyre rash va yoi?* Who are you? *Kyre hirimi?* What is this place?'

Her interest focused on the deep, bursting-out swamp-split in my side. Splashing water around it, she initiated a new age of agony as the needle dug into my flesh again and again, probing and pulling, pushing flesh inwards and sealing the rent with a ragged cross-line of thread.

I forced my mind to think of other things, words: Captain, Mink, sword, dead. I was t over with threads the thickness of cord. sure my own words should feel clearer in my head. Maybe this gash is really serious? I reached to feel at my head, but she shushed me, and pushed my hand away.

A vision to bathe in, I knew I'd remember her quiet smile in the faint light as long as I lived – 'Perhaps even as far ahead as dawn.' I almost chuckled as I said it. A sharp word from her stopped me, and her hands pressed to each side of my head. She chanted a rote of mysterious words over and over, 'Strength... Power... Rua...

Wellness… Unity…' Intermittently, she picked more embedded bits out of my hair, tutted about the skull wound, and repeated the words slowly, over and over, as though I might remember them better.

Caressing my skin; murmuring. I caught the meaning of that, but she returned to washing and digging into the head split, and didn't sound so positive. 'Mould,' she said several times, pulling faces and shaking her head. 'Swamp fungus.'

Whatever that was, it didn't sound good. But she patted and poked and spat into the wound; rubbed deftly. At long last, she bound up the split with a length of sleeve. '*Dreshi* – I feel freshly pained in all places.'

'Kyre?' she asked, then pressed my hand against her face. *'Li.* I am Rua Li. Of the Rua Sisters. Now *drink*.' I took the clay vial that she proffered, and swallowed the contents; a sour-sweet taste with eye-smarting aftertaste. Two more followed, each accompanied by, 'Drink.' Plus another that she poured onto the head binding, repeating her name, 'Li'.

Seemingly finished, she sat and faced me, held my head and stared into my eyes. Again, she chanted, and repeated the same meaningless words, 'Strength… Safety… Loyalty… Rua.' I spoke the words with her, trying to understand their meanings.

'Hui lut? Why do you help me?' I knew there would be no answer – I scarcely knew what I asked in their jumble of words though more of what they said came back to me – Rua. Li. Welcome. Warm. Help. Body. Drink. Come. Give. Some have a reassuring sound to them, but others are harsher: Scoppo, die, hate, kill, blade, bandit, trooper, Captain, Bannerman. What a dreadful gutter-born language they speak.

That soft one-sided smile, and she urged me back to Furry Corner. Her mutter sounded warmly promising as we pulled the skins over ourselves. 'Whether it's the scrubbing or the *medyky*... Or the words, or the smile, but something's making me feel good.'

She shushed me, and settled close. With much repeating, eye and head-touching and a variety of gestures, I thought I understood her meaning – 'I smelled you. In my head. From afar. And came seeking you.' Her fingers trailed excruciatingly along Tubby's long, newly-stitched split across my stomach; and then the other one. She said something – about the wounds, perhaps – or possibly of other things. She repeated everything slowly as if I might understand better. I didn't; but either my wounds, or my future, didn't sound wonderful.

By then she was caressing elsewhere. Her murmurs sounded considerably more approving, as her fingertips delved, and stroked me softly.

Straightway, my... my *something* was rising uncomfortably again. *'Shoh!'* Her fingers curled around me and massaged. My breath taken, I sucked in abruptly as she pressed closer. Unsure why, I tried to find a way through the furs and covers to reach her body. It was a dream of warmth and refuge and delight at the unknown. Uncertainly, I explored... and probed into her softness and intimate places... a smooth curve... a tuft of silken hair. In moments, we were sharing low gasps and murmurs, warm clutches and gentle touches, bodies pressed together, legs intertwined.

I had no idea what this was about, what I should do. I burned in shame and regret for being there, for doing this... whatever it was. *'Kroit!* I wish I'd never started, not had today in my life, not had a life.'

But she knew, guided me, and I was grateful for her dominance, and calmed as she delicately eased and gripped at me, leading me to enter her. So carefully and gently at first, and I was overcome and then I knew… powerfully, and driven. Feeling her tighten and dig her fingernails into me.

'Jeemo! Kyre. Slow… slow.' She urged me, softly massaged and eased. And she wriggled and writhed back at me, impaling herself. We each sighed and thrust back.

**

The exigencies ended, we sank into a torpor, arms entwined. Through the night I tried to ease my agonies in body and mind. 'What have I been doing? How can I not know? Is there some terrible aftermath to this? What will the dawning bring?'

Sick inside, I tried to sleep. At one time, I was aware of troopers at the gates, peering in, talking briefly in ominous tones. *'Ti liuk.* I fear I'll need to be rested for the morrow.'

Somehow, I found her presence deeply comforting, warmly asleep beside me. Occasionally, she nuzzled closer and pressed her forehead against mine, as though passing her inner thoughts into me. Her hands nestled round my head as she murmured the words – perhaps to heal me, or for me to remember, 'Strength… Realm… Loyalty… Rua.'

From time to time, her delicate fingers strayed, and lingered over my muscles and injuries. 'Jeemo, Kyre,' she said, many times, as she stroked me. 'Such power you hold… such strength.'

As the sky lightened, her warmly naked body stirred again, her hands on me, coddling and demanding anew, her voice persuading, encouraging. Her body so supple and smooth, and it aroused me as the night before. My breath came in forced gasps as I explored her inviting softness again, finding she responded to some touches, and to others. And to yet others, as did I, with more urgency.

I believed I knew what to do now, but she surprised me, sliding her nakedness over mine, and pressing intimately together. I had so little understanding of what was happening, permitting her to ease me back, mounting me as she adjusted her position, spearing herself. I adored her, her words, her body, her movements. Welcoming her softness around my hardness.

Lost in the power of the experience, I let it happen, encouraged where I could, and responded as best I might. I stroked at the tactile vision that rode me, eased the furs back and gazed at the unsuspected beauty of naked breasts as she writhed and gyrated on me.

We both gasped and strove in increasing urgency for a dreamlike age, until I burst into her, completely lost in awe and release. That face of splendour, body of utter wonder… ecstasy for mind and body.

'Li,' I said. 'Li.' Knowing there was definitely something infinitely more splendid about women than men.

**

Easing free of each other, I lay still, momentarily sated, my mind wandering over new things. 'I've been dragged out a swamp… butchered seven men… entwined with a woman twice. *Yuaka!* So much going on; all so baffling. My big trouble is *kiri-ya* – I don't know *anything*. I'm filled with confusion; strange people, and words with unknown meanings – Strength… Li… Rua... Safety. She means me to remember these things. To believe them? Live them? Why? What do they mean? Realm… Unity… Loyalty?

‘Why am I here? There must be a reason for being in this world. But it’s lost to me.’ My head wound panged and stabbed, as though awakened by my uncertainty. ‘Did someone, or something, have a purpose sending me here? Did I truly fall through the trees into the mud? Where from? For what purpose?’

From somewhere very close came that same piercing two-note sound that had led the swamp troopers to the gates, now repeated three times. The gates to the compound were pushed open, and four scruff-coated troopers stepped in. ‘So,’ I wondered, ‘what do you plan now?’

Li waved them away. They hesitated, conferred, and turned to the corpses in the corner. Although grimacing, they didn’t seem to be greatly concerned about the ravaged state of them. One trooper searched through the pockets, removed a few pieces of something, and collected the remaining boots and other clothes.

She murmured, and pressed me back down, holding and cuddling me for a moment. I squeezed back, but she was rising, wanting to check the wounds beneath the red-stained bandages. Her expression conveyed a sense of, “Ah well, such a pity.” That faded smile. A regretful gaze, perhaps, as she stood and pulled a karakul pelt around her for warmth.

The darkened bruise that stretched from ankle to my neck caught her attention. She touched along it, pressing tentatively, before moving onto the red-stained bindings across my side and stomach, peeling them off in a time of skin-ripping, crusted blood and deadened flesh. I poked delicately at the stark and sticky slashes – laced with Li’s thick thread to hold them together. Felt sick.

It took long moments to pour something sticky and stinging into the wounds, and to replace the bindings with less-bloodied ones. And then to manage three more swallows of the oily drink as she held my head, endlessly murmuring the same few words, staring into my eyes, as if the message would sink into me and be understood later – 'Strength… Loyalty… Rua… Realm...'

She brought me the salvaged clothing. I sniffed at each piece dubiously, and struggled to pull them on. Li sliced the tethers from my neck and coiled one round my waist. It was almost hidden by my newly-acquired too-tight shirt. The needle dagger seemed to meet with her approval, and she pushed it into my tether belt, putting a finger to her lips. That was clear enough. So wondrous, her bearing seemed less tense now, with bounce in her movements.

'Captain Briand,' she said. And repeated it several times, nodding. Make sure I understood.

I nodded back, 'Captain?' That was the tall one in the braided uniform. '*Kyret?* What about him?

She led me to the open gates. Beyond the gathering crowd of muddy-green troopers stood a thing with wheels, two of the large beasts beside it, a cage on the back. Around it stood a dozen troopers, their uniforms the same dark green as the Captain's. She touched my chest, and waved towards the distant hills. 'Wagon. Captain Briand. Great House. Kyre Go.'

With all her waving and pointing and touching, I gathered that the captain's own soldiers were to take me somewhere far away. He has plans for me? Not a welcome thought – A more ritual, public execution, perhaps?

The mud-and-green regular troopers already in the compound snapped a few words to Li, pushing her away. She paused at the threshold. 'Kyre,' she said. That part-smile again before she turned and in two beats was lost to sight in the assembled ranks of the bannerman's soldiery.

'Rua Li, *Kyrisha.*' I said, feeling more alone and desolate than I had in the swamp. You have whatever you fought the captain for? Leaving me to... what? Captain Gold Braid with his wagon? Or Silver Stripes with his massed troopery?

The nearest troopers turned to me, grinning, one jabbing a goad into my back. I whirled and had the runty little black-haired *vaahto* up in the air by the throat. *'Noiya dammi.* Touch me once more and your throat will gone.' I tossed him away, suddenly aromatic in his fear, and stalked through the gates.

Outside, the forest troopers were suddenly massing before me. I stood for a moment and glared at them, sliding a hand inside the tethers for the dagger. One of my escort spoke, and pointed to the wagon which was barely visible beyond encrowding soldiery. He pushed me ahead, 'Captain Briand,' he said. 'Go.'

A gap opened up as I approached. Each side of me, angry, hating faces jabbered, spat and threatened. Swords raised.

I flexed my grip on the half-hidden dagger and carried on through the reluctantly-opening gap. At a half-dozen paces from the wagon, there was a bellowed command. My way was blocked by a dozen men in an instant, swords outstretched. Silver Stripes was there, shouting orders.

'Ji vaahto, Mink.' Strange how you realise immediately that some events are not omens of salvation.

The darker-uniformed group around the wagon looked at each other, alarmed, raising their weapons uncertainly. Mink angrily repeated his orders, clearly expecting immediate obedience from the Captain's dozen, as well as his own horde. They kept saying *Captain* again and again.

Their protests were to no avail: Mink backed up his demands with a stream of jabbered orders, drawing his own short broad-sword to reinforce his message. A circle of swords was forming around me. 'So much for the Captain's wagon ride through the hills. You can't bear to lose a few useless troopers, eh, Mink, you *Frykerling?'*

The escort party began to back down, swords lowering.

Names were jerked out. A dozen troopers stepped out from the bannerman's ranks, swathed in confident smirks. A swagger to their demeanour, hefting weapons from scabbards – some with heavy broad swords; others with longer, slightly curved blades. *Kroit,* but these look more capable: active fighters, used to scrapping skirmishes. Better chosen than Scoppo and friends, hmm?

Slowly, they spread out, circling all around me. 'This is strange: I should be *kroiting* terrified, and I'm not.' A grim corner of my mind almost chuckled as I wondered: If I'm killed now, will whoever dropped me into the forest swamp be fryked-off? I must be here for a reason – some purpose other than a messy death in the dust of an army camp?'

Lowering to a fighting crouch, I tightened my grip on Tubby's spike-knife as their encircling movement stilled, and they readied for the attack. 'Now we'll see whether I'm bound through the hills to Great House; or do I return to the darkened Vale of the Swamp? *Tri ky mi.* Come on, you pack of *vaahtos…*'

I growled back at them in challenge. *With luck, there'll be a woman waiting for me, wherever I lay this night.*

***

LOST IN TRANSLATION

'Do you fancy me?'

Oh, Phase the Gods! Not now. I kept my head buried in the plaspap documents. Human legs. Small feet – a woman. *Stupid chat-up line, that was. Damn. Thought I was the only hominic hereabouts. Azada's not the best place for us. They aren't moving. Don't look up. Ignore them.*

Steadfastly there in front of me, the feet stayed put. *Go away.* I fervently wished, and ignored them. Waited. They weren't moving, I had to do something…

Eh?' Reluctantly, I raised my eyes from the dataplaz. *Yes, a bloody woman! In a jookya bar, in a dumpy area like this?* You know how sometimes you just feel the doom closing in? This was exactly such a time. *Mustn't lose it. Too much at stake here.* I looked her up and down, more than a tad irritated at being disturbed. 'Fancy you? No. I don't. Go Away.'

Trying to look round the bar without being too obvious – and that's not easy when you're the only one without tentacles, frills, pincerettes and/or carapaces – yeah, a few were looking ominously in our direction. *Froikit, go away, woman.*

Anything rather than look directly at her, or anyone else, I stared determinedly at the news-stream – something about an attack on two tourist troyks just down the road. *Stupid area to be in – the low-life suburbs of Azada, all dust and scrub. The guides should know better than to take troyks through there – or any of the soft invertebrate species. It provokes the locals, after their history together.* The datscreen was saying they were—

'Why not? Some sort of Queedie, are you? Hiding under a stupid SN cap?'

'That's a great way to start a conversation in a bar like the Radiation Sickness, Lady. Now clear off. Whoever you are, I'm busy.' I made it more intense than my usual hiss-and-snarl tone, peering out from under my perfectly fine officer's cap – it's how they know it's me. Another swift glance round again: a couple of avvies were looking down their beaks in our direction – that was disturbing in itself. 'A jookya is no place for anyone to draw attention to themselves, especially a non-humble, human woman. Go away.' But she remained standing while I sat. That was a challenge in itself, as well as ignoring my dismissive wave. A questioning, demanding air about her. *Not today, woman, go away.*

'Why don't you fancy me?'

'Because...' I looked again. 'Koh, koh, I imagine you were attractive once. Now, you've been in the Radlands too long without shielding. Look at yourself – paddled and raddled. So, no, I just don't. Thank you. Please go. I'm working.' I waved her away again, returning to the local news paps.

'Oh. I was rather hoping you'd say "yes", being the only human woman around these parts. Then I'd say you could take me across the Radlands in your wagon. Towards Astyar, travelling as man and wife. And I *would* be your wife – I'd sleep with you for my keep.'

She what? Did I hear her right? I took another look. 'Sorry, Lady, that's not an appealing prospect, much less a viable business proposition. So no. Goodbye.' *Why on Adrom would I want a woman around? Especially out in the Radlands.*

'You know the way. I can't travel alone.'

'So don't go. There's no such thing as "The Way". The whole land is unstable. It changes every day. I know of *one* maybe general direction towards Astyar. But that was yonk-days ago. It won't exist now. Past Spy Point, there's no route, or trail.' *There. My big speech. Now froik off.*

'But you're the only one who can take me. It would cost no more for two.'

What are you froiking on about? A mountain of patience, I stared at her again, *Yeah, rad-faded. Might have been a looker once.* 'There's no logic to that, Lady. I'm not going there. Don't want company when I travel, or drink, or work. Crossing the Radlands would cost my life, plus expenses. Besides, I'm off women.' *Go away: there'll be trouble in here if you don't shut up and clear off.*

'Froikit, woman. You're blowing me here. I've merged in for six days, made contacts and friends with two dozen people, of five different species, and now it looks like I'm acquainted with the likes of you.' Another side-glance. The bubble-heads were pretending not to stare – being polite. A couple of avvies sidled out, muttering, feathers fluttering. *That's Xix and Mogh off my chatting list – after all the bother I went to, learning some Avvie-chitter-chatter.*

'Just standing here and speaking with me, uninvited, you're costing me money.' *If Jokl the Traderman comes now, he'll vanish in a puff of kinsmoke; and another deal would vanish.* 'We humans aren't so common in these parts—'

'You're plenty common enough.'

Great. You want flattening, just say so, stupid. 'We're not so common that they know what we're like. Easy to misunderstand us.' *What a sagger: if I leave, they'll think*

I've been summoned by a higher authority – Me! The original loner. All my work, my deals. Froikit.

I give up; can't leave for at least a half-hour now. 'Fetch me a large cooyuck – just me. Not you.' *The only way to salvage my deals, is by not panicking, let her stay, and pray your contacts aren't going to take this too much the wrong way.*

Returned with my drink, I told her to sit on the floor, beside me. 'We can talk later. Stay there. Don't move. Don't speak. Right?'

She nodded. Sat slowly on the floor next to me and I whiled away a half-hour in quiet discomfort with the weak cooyuck she'd brought.

Jokl waddled in eventually, ignoring the world as he sensed everyone and everything around him. Propped against the stag-rail, he waited while his beverage was concocted and he'd tested it. Eye-slits flickering my way a couple of times. *So. He's brought something. Right...*

'Get out.' I nudged my foot-slave. 'Sit and wait outside the door.'

I thought she wasn't going to comply, so I gave her a harder side-kick and cuffed her ear. *You need a loud thrashing if you can't obey quicker than that.* She went, looking round the bar for whatever had occurred to make me want her out so suddenly. *Silly kibbrit – how to make it obvious you aren't a slave. You'll get a separate beating for that,* I silently promised.

Half a minyn later, Jokl wobbled over, pushing his little soma-cart. It was a sort of life support system in this too-oxygen-rich atmosphere, although I reckon he used it for topping up his alcohol and prinfaric levels as well. I put a hand on his labrum, right between his mandibles. It was always a relief when he accepted my welcome without biting my hand off.

Greetings over, we did a bit of mumbling and examining packets. I tabled my cash. A wad of heavy-gunge slid out his fore-pouch to sit beside my stake. And we haggled over how many gem-stones I could have for that much. He tried the hard and reluctant act, but, the way he was sucking up the prinfaric juice, he was keen for the sale, the swifter the better.

There! Satisfactorily concluded – they were exceptionally high-quality gems that I could resell with no bother. He stayed to chatter for a while, until we noticed Wulett waving his antennae to indicate he wanted my attention. So Jokl shuffled away, and Butterball Wulett – he's a lot fatter than most hrypsids – slid over for his deal. Beautiful – rough diamonds and saffentires, with a few orange-yellow sunstones as well. Rare of such quality these days, so we were both happy that I took them all.

'I like you, Raphaellino Me'Me. Your money good. Not like zippers', or the avvies'. Nobody want their money.'

'And I like you, Wully. Good quality stones. My partner will be pleased to find a home for them.'

She put in an appearance at the door, waving. *You stupid, pushy scroitter.* 'Scuse me, Wul.' I rose and bowed, 'One minyn, please.' Three seconds later, she was flat on her back on the roadway outside, squawking and trying to protect herself from my loud and scarcely-touching-her beating. 'Do as you're told, stupid. You're a slave. You don't look, you don't argue, you don't think. Now sit the shyke down and stay down. I got business to finish.'

Back inside, *Why do women always froik things up? I'll have to stay here even longer now to prove my status over her.*

I'd had a recommendation to meet a threesome of zippers, supposedly with a stash of blue opalite crystals. *Maybe they're in the shadows, watching, deciding about me. Best I don't look round too overtly.*

So that means having more to drink, another nibble and smoke. But, if they do arrive, it could be pay-day times ten. If.

They did. Exceptional deal, too, in quality, quantity and price. It was an old hoard they were releasing onto the market, slowly enough to keep the price up, but enough of them to make us all considerably richer. The deal made the day well worthwhile. Socialised with the zipper-trio for a time, and eventually thought it was okay to depart with my reputation not too wrecked, and a very pleasing day's trading.

I took my leave. 'Seek well.'

'No leaks,' they chorused in response.

***

Finger-clicking to the rad-faded woman on the way past brought her to heel and she followed silently to my powercab. Good mood that I was in – what with the drink and something in it; pouches containing a mix of rough and cut gems and crystals as evidence of two good deals; and a foldbag filled with the zippers' opalites; plus several new contacts and promissories.

Yep. Good mood, I'll hear what she's cribbing about, having spent half the afternoon waiting to put her case. Any damage done by her appearance was probably limited to a loss of time and having her latched on for a time. Maybe she's a good luck button? Sure don't look like one. Right age, wrong radiation exposure.

'You drive one of these?' I asked her.

She nodded. And drove like it was her second time.

Back at my place, I told her to hitch the powercab to the travelvan that I lived in most of the time. There's always someone watching, so it was best if she did it. She wasn't too good at that, either. 'Koh,' we sat with a scuff'n'coff each in the back of the van. 'Let's get straight on what we've just done back there. I don't know what you're used to, but that was a jookya bar – a low-life dive in a run-down part of a perimeter town. And we humans aren't common around here. They don't dislike us: we don't radiate emotions they can figure. The other five species in there have existed longer together, and know how to behave and react with each other; they mostly have similar moodlings. For good and bad, humans're the new kids in the airlock. It makes them wary about our intents, skills, reliability. Some'll bully you, screw you over for a profit, sell you. So we have to go slowly with them, give them time to decide at each stage.'

She was pretty much ignoring me. 'You got that?' I demanded. 'You koh on that? In case there's a next time?' She nodded, reluctantly, I thought. 'Alright – so tell me all about whatever it is.'

'I wish you'd take your tatty old cap off. It looks silly. You're indoors, sort of,' looking round my compact little van.

'I don't do taking off,' I told her. 'The locals recognise that it's me under it. Means I'm open for business. Now…?'

***

Thus, three days later, we arrived at Spy Point, looking down and far away across the Radiation Lands. I took a deep breath on seeing it, as on every occasion I stood here at the start of a trek. Stretching away below us was a mass of ridges and ravines fading into the distance; a vivid patchwork of electric reds, glowing blues and violent yellows. All misted over, beneath a black-lowering sky.

'What you can see down there is our first four- or five-days' travel. Rad suits on all the time. Then it's the Truggh – the shifting rad-sands desert. Followed by the Ragged Mounts – all jumbled rock and vicious little patches still bubbling up, radiating through the whole spectrum.'

'I heard,' she said, 'that the Raggeds were created by one of the biggest catastrophe events that damn-near sterilised this world. Some ancient city or complex was there?'

'I heard the same.'

***

Getting here was fairly simple, making it out of Azada without having to ladle out a real beating for her, although I'd have felt better for it.

Her opening proposal was beyond the borealis. I no-no'd the idea of letting her sexy bits pay for her travel and keep.

'You pay in spendable currency, like all the other dozen or so parties I've escorted across the Truggh.'

'I don't have that kind of money in any form – metal or gems, deeds or cred, artefacts or tronix. I have *this…*' She laid a thick folder of documents on the table.

'So you can't go.' *How obvious does it have to be?* 'What you want isn't a trip to Astyar, it's a prospecting expedition. And you're not even clear about what we'd be going for – what's actually there, or precisely where it might be.'

I spent time shuffling through the dossier's contents. 'There are big problems – all this refers to an area that's at least ten days hard travel away. It's not just over *there*, the other side of the next hill, simply a matter of stumbling on the exact spot you want. The Raggeds are a *Big* place to go searching in, especially after a tough trip through Radiant and the Truggh.'

'This lot doesn't amount to *real* proof of the existence of anything. It's merely a heap of documents and writings, plazpaps and maps with all kinds of notes and markings on them. Maybe they're genuine originals – or might be stat-copies of official records. There's some good fakes around. I know: I did some.'

'You?'

'For tourists. They love'em.'

She regarded her own collection with new suspicion.

'The way you have them sorted,' I carried on pushing, 'they do look like they're all about one specific area – that might be somewhere I know as well as anyone. True enough, there's been rumours for eons, of more intense glowing lights. Possibly with stone, crete and metal ruins. High concentration readings; ground that's extra-tumbled and disturbed, kinda upturned; perhaps roadway surfaces, cables – most of it too broken or chem-rotted to be certain. But the same can be said about a dozen locations in the Raggeds.'

She looked irritated more than dejected, 'I have the maps to guide us.'

So I conceded a little, 'Now, to be honest about it, possibly, there's something in it. I do know an area – that *is* different, and off the unbeaten track, a rocky, low-mountain shatter-zone with a lot of underground activity and severe rad-patches. Very unsettled surface. I'm not sure that this refers to the same region, but…'

***

Perhaps I'd been in a state of semi-euphoria over the deals of the day, and her yappering in my ear. Our eventually-agreed arrangement was fifty-fifty shares in whatever we uncover. She absolutely didn't like that split, and slammed out twice during the row – or negotiations, as I thought of them. I dunno, but it's conceivable I was trying to see the positives in all this. Just a tiny something was occurring to me: studying one of the maps, turning north around to south, a formation seemed familiar. A narrow, rising pass with a high needle-pinnacle on a sharp zig-zag bend. It doesn't exist any longer, and it hadn't been where her documents claimed it to be. It was through a totally different side-ravine into an area of jumbled *karmaki* landscape – rough.

I told her about it, 'But it was to the east of Junction, not the west.'

She didn't want to know. 'If this much evidence exists, it must be right.'

'No, if this much evidence is genuine, why hasn't someone else funded a major expedition long ago, and uncovered it? Hmm? Maybe someone has, and is keeping very quiet about it?'

She had a very firm set to her jaw – stubborn *kurva*. 'Just maybe,' I said, 'don't you think people have been looking in the wrong, nasty, life-ending place?'

Unwilling to listen to Reluctant Raphy, as she called me, that was one of the times she stamped out.

So, I was thinking, *perhaps I ought to go, back in the Raggeds – I'm having flash-backs more than usual. Could see if I get anything specific, I suppose. And it's half a year since I was in Astyar. I ought to pay a visit... it is sort of home, in a way. And Keffy'll be expecting me sometime. That's how partners are – they prefer to remember what you look like, as well as seeing ledgers of how much cash you're accumulating, or draining. But I air-post packages to him for cutting and selling often enough. He knows all the other gem folk up there – the collectors and prospectors; the miners, buyers and sellers.*

She was back at the doorway, exasperated with me, by the looks of her…

Yes, I should go to Astyar. Get spoffed on happy-weed with Keffy and his family. Ha – a right Crusty, he is – definitely has a tinge of coppery blue in his blood. Renew all the other acquaintances. Show my face generally. Maybe go down the coast to Roinstree. Stay there a time – remind myself what it's all about.

'Alright,' she said, 'Fifty-fifty. My info—'

'And my everything else. Alright, 'I agreed. 'I'll go. It's time I was in Astyar, anyway. Besides, the coast up there is awesome.'

'Never been. I wonder if I'd like it?'

'If we reach Astyar, you can find out.'

'Ha, many thankyous for the invitation. If we reach Astyar, I'll hold you to that.'

You have to have your smirking little triumphs, don't you?

***

Now, on Spy Point, at the top of SafeAgain Pass, we could take a long look over the radiation wastelands. Seeming endless rocky valleys and ridges, a few scrubby bushes and tree remnants; not a place to relish going into, especially when all you have to look forward to is a repeat of the last couple of times down that way. 'We'll stay here overnight,' I told her.

'We have another six hours of daylight. We could—'

'No, we couldn't.' I sighed. I'd found out over the past two days that she always argued. I always explain. Then we always decide I'm right. Yet still she argues. 'In five hours we'll be down there in all the purple mist and dust of Pit Valley. From there, it takes minimum three hours to get onto the next ridge, out the murk. So, come dark, we'd be down *there.*' I pointed. 'In the depths of the purple murk. Thus, we stay here. Apart from that, I need to see it at night, from a distance – see where's glowing the brightest—

'Looks nice at night, does it?' Little Miss Sarcasm.

'It looks belly-sucking dreadful. If you have any sense, it'll put you totally off going. About a third of people who see this view at night are deterred from going any further. And a third of the remainers don't get through The Radiant; the first four days, starting with Pit Valley, right down there. It's where most of the glow originates. I need an idea which specific areas we want to avoid; and see if there's any likely-looking route. Now rest. If we're going on, I want to be down there not long after sun-up.'

'Of course we're going. You told me you knew a way—'

'I said *possible* way. The ground changes too often for any even semi-permanent. We have to check every noon and night what the situation ahead is, which way to try next. When you've been this way as many times as I have, then we can discuss it. Not before.'

'You said only a dozen times—'

'A dozen times all the way through to Astyar with parties; more than that on my own; and ten times that prospecting, rescuing, escorting…'

'But—'

'But froiking nothing! Listen. No, *look*. Here. You need to realise how awful this will be. See…' I grabbed a sharp splinter of basalt rock. 'Here's Azada…' I scratched a star on the flat rock we stood on. 'We've spent two days getting here, Spy Point. Down there is Pit Valley, the first tiny bit of at least four days getting through Radiant. You can just make out the end mountain chain – far distance? Yeah – *there*. That whole way, we're at the mercy of shifting ground and radiation bursts before we even arrive at the Truggh Desert – another three or four days getting across there. Only then do we approach the region we believe your maps are focused on – The Raggeds. You with me?'

She was looking blank, disbelieving. 'Stupid kurva. You should be terrified. Even once we get to The Raggeds, we could easily take six… eight… ten days finding whatever we're looking for. If it exists—'

'Of course it exists.' She tried the indignant bit, but I saw the touch of doubt there.

Never mind. I was the opposite, with a heap of doubt, but a touch of belief, too. So it added up to one of us being convinced, in total. 'And it depends on us recognising it, if we find it.'

'*When* we find it, Reluctant Raphy.'

‘Okay. We’ll be positive. *When* we find it, there’s probably ten days further to Astyar.’

‘And that’s why we’re loaded to the dado with stores and gear.’

‘Nope. We’re loaded way past the high mark because it’ll likely take us twice that time. It’s the emergency buffer: we can get stuck; break down; get lost or trapped. And…’

‘What?’

‘Twice before, I’ve met and rescued groups who were stranded. They take a lot of feeding if all their own supplies have gone.’

‘You’re not obliged to—’

‘Of course I am. Everybody going down there knows three things – One, they’re on their own. Two, if you find someone in bother, you help. And three, don’t count on it. Not anything.’

***

She rested, restlessly. Too wound-up-argumentative to settle. I re-checked the water count, the air seals, oil pressures, power levels, and a trill and one other potential disasters.

Hiking back to the point as the light faded to darkness, we sat to watch the colours changing. Looking down, and across, the landscape took on a completely different aspect. The night colours and shapes changed, glowed. ‘Straight down, it’s Pit Valley,’ I said. ‘Everything beyond is The Radiant.’

‘Pitfire!’ she murmured, ‘It’s ghastly… so lurid.’

‘You must have seen the like before? You’re radiation-faded more that I am.’

‘Not here. Southern Glowlands. My father and I prospected for archaeological treasures among the ruins of a previous-civilisation city. Found a lot, but the Vajan Institute kept it all. Paid us off with a few creds and the sickness. We weren't aware of the hotspots thereabouts at the time. Never seen the blue as intense as these, though. Nor any of the red – that's quite something.'

'The red is the volcanic glow from small breaks in the surface, like the ones down there. Or the distant red is from a major lava upwelling that's over to the east. Not a problem for us.'

'But the blue's so intense, among the mist.' She stood to see better down the steep slope before us.

'They're the radiation bursts. Can't see them at all in the day, when we're travelling. 'S why I need to look now, check where the hotspots are. They mightn't be the same tomorrow, but this's the best we'll get. Right. Sleep now. We're up at three—'

She turned, reflection of the radiation in her eyes, a hand coming up, fingers catching the peak of my cap. *No way am I scrabbling round after it. If you're that desperate to get my cap off, go on, look. I hate you; you might well be Dead before Dawn – as the saying goes.*

'Oh, my lord,' she mumbled. 'Oh my.'

I let her look. *You're that curious about what's under my cap? Go on satisfy yourself. Stare all you like. Mangle-Mess, huh?* 'So now you know. Not pretty, huh?'

She fled.

***

Things went downhill after that. We did, anyway, starting down into Pit Valley by searchlight: me and her – Meon, she was called: Meon Suweba.

'Suweba? Don't that mean Longtime? In Vajan?' Damn – I couldn't think of any jokes around that, except, 'Me *not* on Longtime. Me on short time.'

She sneered and said something unrepeatable about, 'Yeah and which bit of you is Shorty?' So I decided to stick with Longtime. The only other company was my one and only real friend – my Powercab SupraYute pulling my stripped-out travelvan. Not that the travelvan was any biggy, 'Sorry about the space, I'm always removing and refitting the extension, different equipment and stuff, depending on where I'm staying or going. And I wasn't expecting a passenger.' I tried withering her, but it was wasted effort.

The downhill was precipitous. Very winding. There'd been two patched-up slips since I was last there. We met a double-track vehicle coming up, small and amateur unregistered. I've seen him before – he's a regular around Azada. It was their obligation to give way to us, and reverse to the last crossout. 'We're going nowhere.'

He came close up. 'I'll push you over the froiking edge.'

Tracked vehicles got a better grip than us and he could do it, too. He still refused to back down. Until I pulled the KK-904 on them and cocked it. Then he shot into back-gear and pulled into the crossout where he should have gone when he first saw us. 'Good mind to report him,' I grumped to Longtime. 'Except there's no-one to report to. Or register with, for that matter.'

'Check the seals round your mask, and wear it while we're down here.' I told her, when we arrived in the bottoms in the gloomed swirls of vapour, searchlight bank on full. 'The cab might leak.'

Three times I had to get out and walk ahead, which means wearing the full outside suit down there. You're bathed in all this blue misty light, and I was waving her up behind me. Real careful. Very slow and steady.

'Froik!' she frightened the life out of me, jerking the cab forward like that. 'You won't last long on your own if you flatten me.' So she was more careful after that. Especially after I pulled the KK on her.

In truth, we struggled through Pit Valley in reasonable time, and climbed the Foreslope – meeting two others heading the opposite way – pair of Pekerjas in a small-dee carrier; and some crate that probably had a zipper crew aboard. You can't tell – they had the pinked-out windshields because of the light.

Now however, there was Radiant to cross, and in the middle of the night, the glow-spots were pretty clear. We compared the new sightings with the map overlays from my last time down here.

'Not much similarity, is there?' she said.

'I wouldn't expect anything else,' I resigned myself to it, took a v-rad drink and a couple of jous pills, and slept.

***

Longtime drove on the better bits and I took the tricky ones, till she was more used to the cab's power torque and little steering foibles. Learning its quirks was never planned as a tuition session on every occasion. It tended to be like when she was driving downhill and the slope had become steeper and steeper.

'Quite a bit steeper,' I agreed afterwards, when the rig had run away with us, and she didn't know how to deploy the extra-wide and extra-grip strakes on the wheels. By the time I'd chased after her, leapt, and pulled the lever, we were doing twenty fps. It took a lot of cursing, skidding and dust-raising panic to bring us to a halt.

'Sorry about that,' I apologised. 'Should have shown you how to use the strakes when we need a better grip.'

Sagging over the steering console, she agreed, back-handed my face – cap gone again – and lurched forward.

'It's unfortunate the crevasse was there.' I consoled her later. 'You weren't to know. And, about the other thing? That was my fault for not explaining about reverse gears.' It would have been hair-raising if I'd had enough hair to erect, sliding to a halt on the edge of the ground-crack. Then re-starting forwards instead of backwards.

'The arrow on the damn lever points back,' she rounded on me. 'So I assumed—'

'That's the way you push it, not the direction the wagon takes.' I was super-patient then.

It was no help when the edge turned out to be crumbly when we did try the real reverse gear. 'We'll have to go forward,' I said, 'and use the track-ramps.' And we did. Extendable road-ramps – I unhitched them from the roof, fitted them into the front mountings and lowered them across the gap.

'We're not driving over that,' she was horrified.

'*We* aren't. You are. We need to unload some of the back-weight first, and I'll stand the far side and wave; and kick the end bits if they start to move about.'

It worked, sort of. We survived. So did most of the supplies we carried across. It was a shame that she tripped and dropped one package of food. We could see it, about a hundred side-splatters down. Broken open and sinking under the cascade of sand and rocks that followed it down. Cost us a day, reloading, finding a way back up to the next ridge, and explaining about the other oddments of equipment that I took for granted and she didn't understand, even afterwards.

***

We pulled up on Fore Ridge. 'I named it last year,' I told her, 'and it's still here. And that, in front of us, is the second half of Radiant.'

'This's the section that was glowing so strongly, isn't it?'

'Yep. We'll stay and watch the glow again tonight: decide on a least-likely-to-be-fatal direction to start the morning.'

At least she'd cut back on the arguing since she'd found it took a lot more driving concentration and route-choosing than she'd imagined. Exhausted, she was asleep well before the glows came. I stayed to watch; opened a flask of Sado's Revenge 50%, and stared at her, at the appalling view across the next section, and into the muddy void all around me.

***

'Why I let this happen,' I mused with the flask, 'I'm struggling to recall – something to do with a pile of documents, private vid sources, codes… All the usual info that wishful folk come out here with. Looking for something in what might have been a ruin… or a cache… a lost mine… unspecified treasure… remnants of whichever pre-civilisation we believe in this time.'

There was a sudden blue flash down below, turning darker and fading to a flickering glow.

Longtime's is typical, but better done than most: she's themed it on accounts of a Half-Known – a particular known event. And then pulled everything else she can find, to see if it fits. And all that stuff is either ancient – pre re-population – or anecdotal. Hers hangs together well because she's picked and chosen which evidence supports her theory, and ditched the rest.

So many other expeditions have searched for rumoured treasure of one kind or another. Using much the same system and evidence. It all depends on each expedition's interpretation; and that depends on their initial idea. 'One heap of evidence fits all theories,' I told the last of the Sado's Revenge.

But this is second tier: the writers of her original document claimed they'd found the actual thing... whatever it was. Recorded it. Mapped it. Catalogued it. Then, of course, got themselves lost on the way back with it – vehicles trapped, buried, whatever. Maybe only one had escaped the Raggeds alive. And she – or he – died not long after. So, naturally, the unspecified treasure was cursed.

Longtime's core evidence is a collection of rad and vis communications to and from a Professor Selman, or probably Salmon – the vocals weren't clear, and nor was the print style – лосось. He was an expedition organiser, and non-survivor. And the transcriptions were non-specific about coordinates, and highly interpretable. I could imagine where it might be – here, there, somewhere else. So many places could fit the descriptions, the pics, and the flashes they sparked in my memories. Big area, the Ragged Mountains.

We had pored over it all, that first night, and a couple of nights since, magnifiers at the ready, earphones locked in, translating sites logged on... maps strewn everywhere. Longtime was convinced she knew precisely where it was – the route *had* to be along this direction, based on her archaeology background, from a possible relic from a maybe-ruin towards Hafflore... as it was once known. Now Astyar.

'Come on,' I pointed out. 'All this from your professor – you couldn't even trace which institution he was from –

or if he was a woman, like as not. Only ever referred to as "The professor". No mention of Central, of any specific place, just "Base". Seems likely to me that she or he is a made-up character to hang a bunch of fantasy stories on.'

All her arguing didn't change the fact that I had far more experience in the Radiation Lands than she had. 'Koh, koh.' I compromised. 'It all makes a sort of sense, to anyone except the most hardened cynic. Like me. I've seen all this kind of thing before.' So we went through it time after time, her Little Miss Optimism; me the conscientious objector with his mind open just a crack.

She was utterly convinced, and I could see why an amateur might be. Some of it was good – probably third- or fourth-hand. But a lot of it was the kind of reproduced rubbish that I'd made up myself, for an ex-friend to sell to the tourists in Central Port. I'm not one for cheating anyone, so I told Longtime, 'I drew this one, years ago. See the name of the ruin site *there?'*

A glance at the map, "Rapha Ruins". 'You bastard.' Followed by a torrent of abuse that included a slapped face, losing my cap again, and coming to understand that I was pretty much the Unprintable Anti-Being with half a head that looked like a froiking radiated froiking curlo froiking fruit. So we didn't chat a lot more that day. She was certain she'd be proved right, "When we get there". And I gave up insisting that some details in her evidence mass could be re-interpreted anyhow the reader wanted. Including me. Some pics and descriptions sure chimed somewhere in my memory depths – probably in the bits of my brain that were missing.

Two more days getting through Radiant Basin didn't kill us. Came close, though. There was a half-day moving through a sunken area of shifting bubble pools that poppled and sucked. Rising blebs as big as the wagon, freezing in the air until they cracked and burst in staccato blasts. Couple of places, they were overlapping each other and I drove the whole way, with Longtime squawking and clutching at every lurch and wheel-collapse as the crispy bubbles shattered and crunched all round us like the minefields on Geddon.

She was as nerve-wrecking as the terrain, but we made it with clean unders, and a much-needed cool-off with a zug-jug over the midday rest-up.

***

'This's The Truggh,' I told her. 'The desert. No distinct boundary. Just as baking hot as the Radiant, and just as radioactive and treacherous. It's merely flatter – no peaks. But we get powerful winds from the west in the hot-dry season, and from the east in the cold-dry season.'

'And which is this? Now?'

'Changeover. The air'll be disturbed for a time. We'll get demon footsteps…' She looked blank. 'Twisting winds, whirling vortices. The dust and heat shimmers just make it seem more like a desert. So some scabwipe called it the Truggh *Desert*. It's four days across here, with different hazards, all the dust holes and shifting glow spots, and the— Well, never mind all that – it's a mess.'

Sure enough, the first day was the expected torment of stinking, itching skin and pouring eyes; raw hands and roasting feet. Several glass-melt areas set the tone: several times, the sodam glass clung to the wheels and bogged us down, and needed to be hammered off when we crawled out at the end of each patch. All day… and the next… and another… I didn't know whether to kill her, ignore her, protect her, or hate her. Mostly, it was a mixture, except for the killing bit – I left that to the fiery lands we were crawling through.

We saw one other Yute – not even a Supra model with a trio of zippers driving back the way we'd come. Couple of hundred lengths away, they didn't veer towards us and stop to exchange terrain info. 'Ignorant zippies,' I said. 'I would have warned them about the bubble patches – they're getting worse.'

There was another wagon half sunk in soft fine sand, like dust. It was in a side channel among a series of long yardang dunes.

I walked across to look inside, 'Could be survivors.'

But there weren't. Three male and a female hrypsid were inside, dead and desiccated. I prised the roof-door open and slipped inside. No notes, no plaz paps or recordings. I took a few ID pics, and left.

Half sticking out the sand was a metal something. I went over, the sand softening underfoot as I reached for it and pulled… my feet sinking deeper. 'Shoik! This's what got them.' Shouting to Longtime for the tow cable, I was knee-deep in mynins by the time she brought it across. And crotch-deep when I managed to catch it and tighten it round my waist.

'Fast as you can, hook it on the front bar. Then back up slowly. Not too quick or you'll rip me in half. You remember which is reverse?'

'Sarcasm ill becomes you, Raphy, especially in your situation.'

Give her that, though. She did well. Slow and steady. The waist-band bruising will probably fade eventually.

'Their wagon? Caught by a rad blast or bogged down in the fine sand and run out of water, I imagine. Whatever.' I didn't like to see reminders like that, but what's to do, except shrug and carry on?

'What did you find, you were going for?'

'Ah, yes. It's in my pouch, a metal ceramic tube with some corroded protrusions, and screw holes – a fitment from something, I suppose?' I showed her.

'I've seen similar in the Southern Glowlands. An engine part, we thought… *that* end probably attached to a power inlet.'

'Mmm, yes, maybe. Could be a V-type hot-fluid pump. I'll stash it, check it later.' I stuck it in the cabinet with the other oddments I'd accumulated over the years.

'What on Adrom is all that lot?' She was right behind me. Made me jump.

'Oddments, from over the years… It's koh – look through them if you want – that was Corrianne's bangle… the coins are from Mi'Davv, where I used to live… that's an oil seal that burst in the Bleaklands one time – froik-near killed five of us. That's a huge raw diamond in the resin block…'

'A hand-gun, is that?'

'Relic. Rest preserved artefact I ever came across.'

She took it, turned it over, 'In six years in the Glowlands, we never discovered anything this well preserved. You have all the provenance for it? It's worth a fortune.'

'Not to me. Can't remember where I found it, anyway. Somewhere before my head copped a bad one.'

'That a pre-civ face mask? Flask of something? Bunch of frazzled hair… Oh Yort! Yours? With skin?'

'You must have saved some things you found?' I switched the topic.

'No. Weren't allowed. Didn't need to. We thought we owned it all, but Vajan and Central claimed it and paid us off. Practically deported us.'

We sloshed back the vits and antis; injected the a-radiation dose twice a day; sluiced down three times a day; wore rad suits virtually all the time we were outside the SupraYute or the T-Van; sprayed on the liquid skins and had ten minyns in the detox soak-suit every evening. That was as far as the personal chemistry went. Apart from sniding. It was work. Slightly irritating and unwanted work, at that, and I pleaded with the Gods to get us swift and safe through the Truggh and into the Ragged Mountains where we thought her detailed maps began.

We did talk about the destination, but mostly, we were avoiding too much definiteness and detail: we had differing opinions about the exact nature and location of some of the features. No point bringing it all up in advance, while Longtime was becoming less argumentative, and more capable. She was still eager for the whole big new adventure, constantly sorting through her wodge of evidence, and rebelieving every word and pixel. Possibly, I thought it wasn't too dreadful to have somebody aboard who was semi-capable, rough round the edges and the middle, and more radded than me – apart from my head bit, naturally. So a couple of times I grouched when I didn't especially mean it, and she knew, and she stopped moaning and condemning all the time.

At least I'm used to The Truggh, and the cab and van were me-designed for these lands, with a three-thousand gayon tank of water, nuke power plant, and a heat exchange unit with aircon. So it was normality for me, not torture

So, scorching bad as the days were, the cool, air-conned nights could be liveable. They made up for the slogging eye-stinging days. On occasion – every night, in fact – she stood open-mouthed at the skittering glow-patches in the area ahead, 'We're not going through *there* tomorrow?'

'Yes,' I'd say. 'There's always radiation, hidden in the sunlight. So we watch now – get an idea of the movement pattern. Work out a best-route.'

She understood that alright – it was how she'd been over-radded in the Glowlands – unseen and unknown radiation areas where she'd worked.

The odd bits of sleep I had were mostly induced – the pills, more than Longtime boring me with her latest idea about the fabled location. We laid out together, usually stripped pretty much down and ignoring each other.

'You need to get your skin open some of the time,' I told her, and left my cap off when I mattressed. Yeah, it was more than bearable at night with the heatex and the aircon giving the whole shubunker, us included, the opportunity to cool off, rid the wagon and stores of built-up heat. And she was tolerable company when she wasn't fixed on her dossier hoard.

***

A couple of times, we rested up when we saw whirlwinds through the dunes or rocks towards us. We did get caught in the side-wind of one, and it was a mite un-nerving. 'They can be devastating. If you see one before I do – you yell, and we anchor down. You press *that*… and *that*. And we get bolted to whatever's under us.'

'Sounds like you learned a lesson there?' she asked.

'Yeah… You don't want to know.'

She did, 'Come on Raphy, we never had whirlers in the Glowlands. Tell me.'

'I was caught by a twister years ago, when I was merely the local liaison for the on-board zippers. Personal guard, hired to keep indigenes away – there'd been a lot of bother with raiders thenabouts.'

'Oh?' She looked out the cab's screens.

'Not now. We ambushed a pack of them the year after. Lured them into a mine where they believed we'd hit a rich vein. Wiped them out.

'But that was after. With the twister, it turned our tracker over on the road out of North Camp. Rolled us at least a hundred lengths down the slope into a dust trap. Four dead – six zippers and an avvie; two humans were cripped bad; didn't make it. Me and Kos the engineer were full-strapped in, and crawled out. Walked three days. Slept outside in suits. Spent two deccas under treatment; cost me a fortune. Went right off whirling winds, too.'

'Powerful things.' She was taking it in.

'Need to respect the whirlwinds, every time. They can suddenly focus into a point, and if that hits you, you're toes and tits up… er… scuse me.

'I went back with a recovery party. But it had been looted already. The non-human bodies had been taken; for funeral rites, I imagine. The two humans were left. The wagon would have been recoverable, but some engine parts had been looted, the compartment left open – corroded…' *The humans had corroded, too, uniforms thinning, bones crumbling, crystallising. They shouldn't have done that – froiking zippers.*

***

Yeah, we talked, nights. Me and Longtime – Like she said my name sounded like I'd won a raffle – 'Raphaellino Me'Me. You're about the last person I'd think of as a prize.'

'I'm from Mi'Davv,' I told her. 'We all have names like Raphaellino Me'Me. I had a brother, Monticello Ne'Ne. I never claimed to be a prize anything – Prize idiot, maybe, with Corrianne.'

Seems she had come to me because somebody I once vaguely knew thought I was disreputable and desperate enough to take her into the Radiation Lands. All through Radiant, Truggh and the Raggeds.

'Besides, you were the only human doing it. Can't imagine why anyone chooses this kind of life.'

'Why? Dunno – lose myself, maybe, after Corrianne. There were a few others, men like me. What's to say? They didn't make it, one way or another. Like I said, humans are rare in these parts. Never seen any women going out as individual hunters. The locals – all four common species hereabouts – have some attitude towards their own women. Basically, they don't take them seriously. Plus – the few toughies who did try it...? They weren't toughie enoughie. No more than the men.'

'Why do I do it? Why not? Sure, folk can fly across, or drive all the way round. But some tourists are the hardy death-brushing sort. Plus prospectors; archeols; scientists; people of all species with something to prove or discover. All sorts. I get along with the languages, and the people, for the most part.'

'Regard yourself as an ambassador for humanics, do you?'

Had to laugh at that, 'Me? Disreputable and desperate ambassadors nowadays, is it? I have a decent reputation among the miners and dealers in Azada for being fair in my prices, and reliable. Disreputable? Sure, why not. But desperate? Not me. I have my own cache, lodged very safe back home.'

‘So what do I ask you next? Where’s home? Or why do this? You trying to kill yourself? Ha…’ She thought she saw something in my expression.

‘Home is here, in the back of my cab’n’van. Or maybe up the coast past Astyar; I got a place there. Kill myself? No… I… I—’

‘Why do you hate women so much?’

‘Eh? Where did that come from? You been slopping my flasks back?’

‘No wife? Woman? Too cussed to be tolerated. Never settled?’

I shrugged. ‘You think that? I don’t hate women. I expect you’re about right – I’m too cussed. Had a Fullwife, Corrianne. We lived on Mi’Davv. I was an engineer; any kind of engines. I’d had the full memos, saw an opp here on Adrom, so we emigrated. She was fine with it, encouraged me. Hi ho… she was something else. Her and my kids – three. New life here; with my skills, I had good prospects. Even if the planet isn’t the most beautiful.’

‘And you end up here? On your own? Doing this? In the worst place on the whole planet? A Radiation Roamer? What happened?

‘I… my fault. I started testing, repairing, modifying the engines; big ones – water, oil, air, power. Then I wasn’t working only on static engines any longer. Some were fitted into heavies – the huge industrial machines, speed machines, all terrainers. I got hooked on the outdoors engines. Big ones, fast ones, new ones – I was helping develop and test them. It started to get too rough for Corrianne – this planet, this region, the life, me, especially me. She ran… took the kids back to Mi’Davv.’

Like I’d tell the truth? She took a fancy to a merchant who was visiting on a trade mission from Smartass or

Somesuch planet. Vanished, all of them, one day when I was down the depot wrestling with a Mark 4 hot-gas pump.

'I'd never been anywhere in the Radiations before she left, but they were testing engines for use out here - high risk of breakdown, high engine wear. They needed a repairman on board. I was in demand because I'd worked on modifying some of them. So all that kind of work just took off after they'd gone.'

Why would I bother any longer, after Corry and the kids had gone? So I took the risky jobs – I was even inside one motor when they ran it, to see what the beiro valve was doing when it cut out. The money was good. I was surviving... didn't much care... But Longtime don't want to know that.

'I went my own way after a few years. Better payoffs from prospecting, escorting, private testing… all sorts… I got into things.'

'But you're not telling me what?'

I had to laugh at that, 'I can't remember half of what I was doing.'

***

'The cap?'

Wondered when you'd ask about that. Almost managed another laugh, and a shrug. 'I pulled a woman out of a mess, down in Abileet. Officer off some visiting ship. She'd dropped down from orbit for a day's sight-seeing on her own. In a right clanging mess with a pack of locals and their livestock at an FT market. She would'a been dead in about ten seconds if I hadn't grabbed her. Seems funny now, but it was a mite desperate then, holding them at bay, explaining about human ignorance and ill manners – didn't tell her I said that.

'But she knew, said. "How can I ever repay you?" You know, how women do, and don't mean it. "You could give me your cap," I said. It was smart then – white and midnight blue.'

***

Yeah... the driver of the whirlwind wreck, too. Woman. Sharp tongue on her. Neck broke in the rolling. Should'a had the strapping on. I kept telling her. Expedition leader was a woman, too. Did whatever she wanted. Never listened. 'I only hired you to protect us from raiders,' she said. 'Not from ourselves.' Good looker. Well distant from the likes of me. Till she was pierced through by a steel rebar in the wreck and she knew she wasn't going to make it. Stayed with her a day and a night, me and Kos. It was the two women's bodies we went back for... them and the wagon. Looked really bad like that.

'I should'a made them listen,' I told Teedy when we saw the remains.

'Yeah, you should.'

Why would I want to get close to a woman again? After that? Didn't save'em.

Longtime was staring at me.

'What?'

'I asked, about your head. How you did that.'

Yes, I could have denied, protested, shelled-up. No... lifted the cap off and scratched at the crusted mess. I could get a hair-mat on it, but what for?

'I got caught outside. Don't know the exact spot – it's changed, anyway. I think it was back near where we were on Day Two.'

She looked pissed with me, 'Do I have to prise every detail out of you?'

'No...' I surrendered. 'I was heading back to Azada. Been testing a Heavy-Max engine in a Bigrig when I took a call about one of the other rigs that had conked. Overheated crossing a new-crust area, and started sinking. My rig was too heavy to go on the crust, so I hand-dragged a line out to'em. Rigged it round the front bars and started winching'em clear.

'Bit of a struggle, gentle, slow. He gets his engine started up and he's coming at me faster than I'm reversing away. He's coming past me, still with the cable attached. He didn't want to risk sinking again, I suppose. But he's gonna twist my rig round. So I franticked and leapt out to unhitch.

'He hit another thin patch, I guess. Next thing I know, he's going over on his side – away from me. Tracks flailing, kicking up the molten stuff underneath. Dollop hit me in the head. That was it. Over in a dozen seconds.'

'And the other rig?'

'Sank. I didn't see it go. I was out, burning. Managed to crawl into mine. They'd gone – Driver was a man – two passengers were women. I pushed the 'mergency call, managed to pull back onto the trackway. They found me the day after, and they weren't happy at losing a rig, new engine and three-and-a-half people.'

'Half?'

'Half my head, the half that remembered things, that recognised people, remembered where I'd been… I get mixed up flashes sometimes.

***

The Truggh behind us, and two long, hard days into the Ragged Mountains, a soul-sapping struggle against precipitous slopes up and down, or working across the face of them; ravines to jiggle across or go round; fire crevasses and glowing bubble pools. The Raggeds have them all.

We were closing in on Junction, where there'd been a major split in the land. I still thought the right fork, and said so. Longwise was convinced it was the left. So when we came to the split-off point, we both knew there was going to be a row.

There wasn't. It was her expedition. All her work; her evidence; her life of the past year or more. She had her arguments all lined up waiting for me – a barrel full of archaeological backups. The past two days, she talked incessantly about details of the topography of our target area – about which she only knew what a few dozen maps and aerial pics and vids told her. The notes and markings, and voice recordings. Plus her ideas about what the stash might be.

We pretty much agreed that it's not a mine or super-rich vein, which left us with a miner's hoard, stolen gems, a wagon or cellar stuffed with relics, maybe something technological from the pre-arrival days. Perhaps the Salmon expedition? Or a fairly intact building from the ancient days? It could be documents from that time? Or some kind of recordings?

She was all set to get hysterical about it, even threatening to get out and walk. As if. But even trying it could kill her. But I'd already decided I had to let her have her way. Maybe 10% chance she's right. 10% it's me. 80% there's nothing for either of us to be right about. So we turned left at Junction.

'We'll give it four days,' I said, when she insisted that her target area was only a day and a half away. 'Any longer, we'll be running too low on supplies.'

'More than enough.' She was glad not to fight for it.

***

We took her route, steep up a valley.

It was looking increasingly promising: there were traces of a possible ancient road, slab sides of maybe buildings. Several landpoints seemed to be very much like her pics and maps.

We enthused about every detail we found that agreed with her dossier.

And spent six days scouring the focus area, and one more doing a swift wider survey for anywhere nearby that looked hopeful.

Nights, we spent in increasing desperation and despair.

I came to my senses. I'd let myself be convinced that this was the right area, that we were finding the right features, that it was here somewhere. Merely a matter of looking in the right way, in the right place.

'We have to face it, Longtime: "it" isn't here.'

She didn't like it, wanted to spend longer there. Scout wider. 'It *must* be here. There's nowhere else, the topography's changed. It's just a matter of looking in the correct area.'

'We've already spent too long here. Our reserves are low. Look at all your data – we can't get a consistent match because you chose it all to suit this place. Because you saw some initial coincidence of form and distance, timing, age of reports, names you semi-recognised. I've been looking through all your stuff yet again, and I reckon it's from three different major places. One lot, I've no idea about – not in the Radiations at all. Someone got them mixed? Accident, deliberate?

'We need to sort them out for ones that are obviously here, on the west side, and discard them. We've checked them out for the past eight days. And they're out.'

***

Downhill, and trying to regain some time, we were only a day returning to Junction. Not that it was much of anything to call Junction – there was nothing there, 'One time,' I told Longtime. 'There was a big 'crete base and parts of a building. Between the archeols and the radiation spread, the only sign of it now is a corner of the base, over that way. Slowly being buried by rock falls from the cliffs.'

Forbidding sort of place. Deep and dark, with the main route going south to north, the way we'd come. 'My thought,' I said, 'was to try the side chasm – that way, eastwards. Up the offshoot. Some of your pics could be along there – except they'll have changed since then.'

'We'll try it.' She was desperate.

'Supplies are getting low – the supplements we lost going over that chasm. We're fine for water and general foods.'

She was getting all set for a massive sulk. Blaming me for going her way for the past days, when I'd known we were wasting our time.

'Koh, koh. We could give it three days. No more. We'd need to be back here on the fourth at the very latest.'

Fired, and filled with new zeal, she had me behind the console and heading into the Karaki. 'No,' I said. 'I'm not desperately worried or reluctant: we should be able to make it. And it's worth a look.' *If only as a recce for future reference. She'll strangle me – now or later – if I don't do as much as I can. And I reckon there's perhaps a twenty percent chance now, counting the ten percent chance that hadn't been the other direction.*

***

She heaved the cab'n'van up onto a solid ledge that first night. 'Good progress, Longtime. Y' driving's good. Lot of practice, huh?' Course, she took that as a patronising insult.

'Lemme go over all this stuff again,' I said. 'and think in terms of this place. It's supposed to have been a centre of population in the Pre-Civ Era, but not one that spread far. Latest idea is that this was a massive research facility of some kind – with a city-sized complex of housing, parks, recreation all around.'

'Something went awful wrong.'

'Didn't it just?' Looking round at the devastation that surrounded us as the darkness settled – revealing two patches of glowlight – a small area close by our rear end, and a much larger one that we'd come through. 'It didn't set the alarms off, did it?'

'I'll check'em when we get somewhere. Anyway, this area's never been properly explored with any system, even the satellite mapping's blurry and poor. The radiation sends the readings and pics off the scale. Drones drop out the sky. The stuff supposedly from here was proven fake.'

'The four original species around here,' It was Longtime's subject of expertise, 'vanished with the Rad Event, whatever it was – Civil war? Experiments gone wrong? Off-planet invasion? Maybe scuttled their city when they left? Maybe some vast off-world craft opened fire on the planet, and wanted to make extra-sure of this particular place? Something sure screwed half a continent round the plug. Deeply screwed, like nowhere else. And what was here before is anybody's conjecture. Maybe there were buildings. But in this terrain and levels of radiation, who's going to come and look?'

‘Well, *we* are. And your Prof Salmon did. I’m thinking more and more that it was this region. Some of your evidence fits this area better than the west side. So let’s see what’s left, and we give this a go?’

‘Yes, yes, we already decided that.’ She shuffled across to see.

I spread the Karaki maps and pics out. ‘I put these marks where I thought some of your pics might be of. Maybe a couple of the verbal accounts are relevant: there’s a mention of Square Head, which is the name of a mountain near here. And I’m thinking *this* view is from the Coutree direction, not from *here*… and *this* one’s got its north and south mixed up. We’ll probe further along here, and it could be any of the next three side-ravines, on the left.’

***

We tried, and we struggled and went out in suits, explored side chasms and onto high ledges to see better and take readings. Found a couple of degraded metal beams, ‘High quality to last so long in this environment.’

Over two days of exhausting searches, I was becoming as obsessed as she had been over the west side. ‘It *has* to be here somewhere,’ I was ranting. ‘If it exists.’

‘You know how stupid that sounds?’

‘Of course I do. But we’ve been too long over this whole thing. We don’t have any more time, Longtime. We have to be gone from here before we’ve bottomed out on everything. So, tonight, we need to be back in Junction, which means driving solid from now, and no more stopping till we’re clear of the Rad Lands. *Shukk!* What the kroit was that?’

‘Something froiking big hit the van.’ She was on her feet, eyes and mouth popped open.

‘Felt more like the cab. I’ll go see.’

Suiting up is a pain at that time of the early night, when nothing's cooled down to bearable, but I went anyway, and took a lamp out to see what had jolted us.

***

'A rock the size of the table dropped off the cliff face and slammed against us,' I reported back, grabbing a flask of Sado's. 'Looks like it's froiked up the rear wheel of the cab, this side.'

'How bad?'

'The wheel's partly off the rim. Twisted off-centre. Won't be able to change it here. Don't have a spare, anyway.'

'Why the froik not?'

'A wheel that weighs a quarter-ton? And needs a machine shop to extract and refit? Yeah, right.' *No point taking it out on her...* 'Koh, I'm sorry. I can maybe hammer it back in a semblance. But…' She wasn't going to like this, 'there's also a split in the side of the stores compartment. The shielding's exposed. I'll need to patch it, pack it, stop the radiation spoiling the stock.' Truly, I wanted to scream and rant and kick and fist the walls, but, 'I need to repack the wheel bearings and seal the oil leak. And reinforce the shielding before we lose any more supplies. I'll move some of them away from that side of the compartment if I can get at them. I'll have to see if I can straighten the plating out, if it isn't buckled too much.'

It was. Buckled badly. I could enter the stores part, but couldn't move any of the fixed equipment out the way to fit any shielding plates behind it, and it wasn't possible to shift the food containers to the other side, either.

Back outside, there wasn't much I could do, not with a froiking great rock-plus-fragments against the wagon.

Apart from try to hammer the plating back straight. I couldn't. Not completely.

Longtime was out there, next to me, suited up, 4H prise-bar in hand. 'We need the rock out the way, Raphy. Maybe we can move it, both heaving?'

We could. Froik-of-a-lot of effort, grunting and straining, but we did it. 'Koh, you get back in and sluice down straight away; take the supps.' I stayed out and kicked and hammered the wheel rim back in place; welded the burst rivets back. Not too well, but it was the best I could do under the arc lights. 'The strakes won't deploy again. I'll pray for easy terrain. Froiking wheel. It's not a permanent fix, Longy. But it should do us. We'll be fine.' I didn't even sound confident to myself. Shaking, blurred, hands weren't helping, either. *Too much of the outside's getting inside. Radiation in, me out.*

Back in the van, I needed to change, and to rest. We both did. But rest wasn't going to come, 'We have to be out of here, Longtime. Could be more rocks falling anytime.'

Froikit to the stubs! We're froiked up. After all this time and effort. I swept the paps and maps aside. *Froikit! Everything wasted. I really thought... Come on, calm down. Can't take the steering in this temper. Damn paps scattered all ways round on the floor. Clear this lot away.*

'Hello... What's this? That looks diff— It's the wrong way up. That's the top. North.' I turned it all ways. 'Longtime? This aerial's the actual site, close in. Not the area. See? The layout looks similar. We got the scale wrong. That's, I dunno, somewhere.' I dug in my mind. *Where? I've seen it before... Have I?*

'Longtime? These paps, see here? This's the wrong way round. It's a site that used to be – might still be – that last tributary ravine. The twisting one where I said there used to be an arch across.'

'So?' She peered at the pic.

'This is the arch, collapsed now. These pics have the same references, same codes. This's the area we want. Definite.'

'Right, but who's to say if anything's here?'

'Koh. Yes. But this is the spot it refers to.' I knew it. Complete certainty.

'Back up that ravine we covered yesterday?'

'We didn't go far enough along. We need to return.' This was so clear. I had this tenth-of-a-second memory flash of some place.

'But the wheel? The stores?'

So now she wants to slam the brakes on. 'You want to know for sure about all this, Longtime? One way or the other? We could be up there by noon. You never taken a big chance before?' *This is me talking? To take a risk like this? Sure – ten times every trip – on my own.*

She was up for it. In ten minyns, we'd eased away from the rock and started down the valley, aiming to cut back up yesterday's failed exploration, past the fallen arch. That was a total nightmare – I was getting more dizzy, blurry spells – that was rad overdoses. And faint, fading spells – they were the lack of supplements and re-vits. 'Getting the wagon back down here is going to be so much worse.

Massive rocks jumbled and shattered. It was as far as we'd ventured the day before. Difficult going over the tangled heap, *The wheel'll be lucky to survive this...*

Two hours beyond it, *We're there. This is the place.*

Paps out, we checked, pored, decided. Yes. Suit on. We went outside, stumbling round, comparing rocks and cliffs with the paps, recalling the voice descriptions. Rechecking the maps… *It's here somewhere. Very close.*

I was getting well past desperate. *If we don't find anything now, we're sunk for good. There'll be no coming back. No staying longer. Don't know if the stores are getting dosed with radiation, damned split panel. Will the wheel take us that far back?*

'Raphy? Raphy.'

I went over to where she tottered, hot-eyed and gasping in her suit. 'There's something over there, under the overhang. See the metal? Looks like a wagon top.'

It was. Not much showing, a roof-rack for ramps and shields. 'Sure isn't Pre-Civ. It's modern-ish.'

We slaved for the best part of an hour, clearing rocks and sand from enough of it to be sure. 'Salmon's expedition?' she wondered aloud when we could see the front and partly down one side. No-one in it. No corpses. That was a froiking relief – I hate to find bodies; makes me dream ill for yonks afterwards. Clearing more sand and rock, we found, 'Raph. There's another vehicle here, butt up behind it.'

I looked. We cleared ash and boulders away. It was part inside a cave.

'They took shelter from something…'

'Eruption?'

'Trapped by a rad burst?'

'Engines? Insanity? Landslip?'

'Fuel?'

'Or water?'

'Whatever it was, if this was the prof's expedition, there was only one survivor known to have escaped. And she—'

'Or he—'

'—didn't last long after… head injury… delirious. I heard some cordings, but they made no sense. Supposed to be maps, too. No sign of them since. His rescuers couldn't make out what any of it meant, much less where it all was. He almost certainly died of injuries of rad sickness. Disappeared, anyway—'

'He was probably kidnapped to force him to tell, if somebody believed in it.' Seemed more likely to me.

'Whichever, it was all forgotten in some other crisis of the day. It was never clear what they'd found—'

'If anything.'

'But snippets turn up in the recordings from time to time… some overlooked notes or markings on maps. And once, someone came across a coin in an evidence envelop, and the code number was traced to a day-log that was attributed to the prof. No other record of when or where it was from; not when it was made, or when it was found.'

'Could have been from any expedition he'd been on, then? Or organised and sent students on?'

'We don't know if he existed, much less if he ever ran expeditions – private or uni.'

'He, or she, *did* exist. I spent the best part of a year gathering all my info together.'

***

We levered a side panel open and Longtime squeezed inside. Dark in there. Torch concentrating the light into the back section among packing cases and bags. She vanished into the rear. Heard her scuffling and cursing. Saw a few flashes and flickers of vids. 'Longtime, come on. We need to move. What you found? What is there?'

She was back, little face agog, 'A froiking treasure-pit, Raphy. This's it. *It.* Ancient times stuff. The expedition found someplace intact. There's docupaps, coins, vids. This's the best *ever*. Could be a whole new perspective on Pre-Civ times. Like a museum in here.'

I didn't hear much more. 'You've taken pics, vids, samples?'

She nodded, I took hold of her, 'Out then. Now. We need to reseal this, and reach the cut before dark – too many random rad spots up here.'

***

'We were doing so well,' I said, clambering out, ready-suited. The wagon was almost on its side, working our way down the fallen arch debris. A rock hadn't taken our weight. Dropped. The wagon with it. The wheel had given way. We'd lurched sideways. 'We're propped against a rock wall at forty-five degrees.' I radded in to Longtime. 'Stay inside for now. I'll see what I can figure.' I desperately needed to weep and rant and pulverise the whole Rad Lands Region.

But no. Sanctified self-control through all the internal ranting. 'We can do this, Longtime. It'll take maybe a day. But we've got to do this. Must. Or so. *Froik! Damn.* I need you to stay in the wagon.'

'Why? What's happened?'

'I just spilt my suit wide open. I slipped; it ripped. I can feel the valve on the back – broke the null-rocker. So you stay in, and I work. This's get-out-able.' *Like one in ten chance.*

She didn't ask. I didn't say. We both knew it was a distinct "maybe" on getting out. Salmon's crew hadn't managed it. Their bodies were likely around there somewhere.

Before night, we'd hitched the front bar with a cable, run it round a solid boulder at the extreme limit of its length, and heaved ourselves off the prop-rock. With much trepidation in such a precarious position, I crawled under, and worked on the wheel until I nearly burned the only suit we had left, 'I'm calling it a day.'

'A foul day.'

'We've survived.' And we sank onto the bedmat together, asleep within the minyn.

***

The whole of the next day working on the wheel. I managed to straighten it. Mostly. But broke a finger that was in the way when a mounting bolt sprang back too far. One pouring with oil, the other with blood, I had to bind them both up. And weld the wheel stabiliser at the right-ish angle. Repack the bearing and pressure-up the seals. 'It might hold,' was the best I could promise. 'It'll need nursing.'

We remained there another night, escaping the following dawn with utmost delicacy on the cable and winch.

We gained Junction by glowlight – it would have been dusk elsewhere.

I was really feeling the effects of the lack of supplements by then – standard supplements, anti-rads and re-vits – sarrs. There weren't enough for both of us, *and I'm not going to lose another woman out here. Stuff the supplements, I've had rad poisoning before. She looks as if she's more in need of them than I am… I'll do without. Have a look for the old medications. The cug'm-stock, as we used to call it – crumbly, useless and gone mouldy.*

We were a bit desperate on supplies, too – the water tank had been leaking since the rock-hit; and the stores compartment was showing radiation levels that were too high – that froiking rock again. So the food was tainted. The air was becoming polluted: the aircon was clunking and labouring too much to cope. So was I. And the water leak… Froik, I was too dried-out to notice anything.

'Outside, I'll wear the suit. You stay in. When we're both in the cab, you have to wear it, in case there are slight leaks – it'll keep their effect down.' *Can't let her become too ill. Froikit, she's tough and determined, but nobody beats heavy rad doses – on top of what she's had before. I gotta try to get one female rescuee out the Rad Lands.*

I found the cug'm stock – I could never throw anything away. *Maybe they'll help. Maybe. Not counting on it.* The water didn't seem too bad. The skin burns I could hide with the xefudi cream. *Not too good for the long term, though. Damn medibox labels kept blurring… couldn't prise the tops off the packs.*

***

Longtime was surviving. That was main. She drove. I drove. She drove best: I wasn't seeing things so great. Her face, maybe, like the Whitemoon light on Caladas as she took the steering column. *Yeah, I've got to put more effort into getting this one back to people-places.*

Her driving was definitely better than mine sometimes. I was getting careless. Didn't read the slopes, the rocks, the rad patches. Damn, I'm getting radded, de-hyded. Can't lose another. Too many rescues gone wrong; men died; women. I was having visions of *her* face, in the twister wreck… how her body had been when we went back. *How superb she'd been before, physically. A kurva, she'd been, but beautifully-built.*

Days on end, easing and crawling through the ravines, over the rocks and crevasses. So careful, painstaking, pointless. Brightly glowing nights and slightly glowing meals, *We're going to rot here, whatever we do. End up like the others... crumbling, or sinking in fire.*

Froikit, I'm getting weaker. Must survive. Get us out of this.

'Ahead! See? Top of the rise... it's the trailway.'

'The right one?'

'The only one.'

***

Dark coming on, I slumped over the console, 'A better day, Longy. We're out the Raggeds... route to Astyar. Clear run through wild dry country, level or rolling. The road improves from here – easier on the wheel.'

Better land – livestock farms on greener lands - cattelyas and zeepaks. Crops. *Road's fading, shimmering. I'm seeing nothing. So close. Froik the stars, I didn't get it right this time, either, I'm radded out...*

***

Eyes hurt. Deep inside. Ache throbbed into pulses of agony. Nothing to see. All blackness. I'm not dead. *Is that hoping or cursing at the thought?* Dumped on the roadside. A ditch somewhere. Feel the rough gravel under me. Can't move. Not a muscle.

Night? Paralysed? In a ditch?

Eyes burning. *That's the rad; so's the deep ache. Froikit – I failed again. Damn survived. I'll get it right one day – save somebody and go out on a win.*

***

I know that smell: tri-septic and excessively fresh. Aircon gone mad. Astyar hospital's the only place that smells of salt air. We must have crossed the salt flats. Don't recall, do I? 'How'd I get here?'

'You were brought in.'

Yoik! I must have said it aloud – a voice came through the blackness. A doc's voice. Weird talking to a disembodied voice. The docs all have that tone, they're all hrypsids – ugly devils. Just as well I can't see. 'Doc Uffud? Astyar H&D?'

'Of course. Nice to see you again, Humal Me'Me.'

'Wish I could say the same, Uff. Who brought me in? Woman?'

'No. Your rig was found in a roadside ditch out past Sellar. I imagine one of you veered off the roadway. I understand it's suffered a variety of dents and scrapes, buckles and bows. There was a woman with you. She's gone.'

'Gone?' *Froiking damnit. She can't have died on me. Not another. Not Longtime.* 'She was worse than me? When? Was she alive when you found us?'

'Avvie farmer found you. He called here. She was alive, yes. Gone now.'

So quiet. So black. Empty.

'She wasn't too bad.' Uffy's voice wandered around me. 'We re-boosted her sarrs and supps. She was dried out and non-nourished, but basically well, for a human. I told her you'd recover. She's left. Charged her care and recovery to your account.'

Left? Whaffor? She's cleared off? Deserted me? Can't do that... Need her... just found her... 'Need to get out of here, Uff... find her...'

Could hear him laughing. Me panicking. 'Don't fight. You're under para-sed. She said she was going to the carateera, for food, clothing. Somewhat ragged – both of you. I told her you'd recover, "He always does," I told her. "Survivor King, he is. Prah Samma, we call him round here. Oiking legend around here – always looks worse than the time before. Always recovers." Don't you, eh?'

'Yeah, right. Like I feel now, huh? I'm wrecked.'

'Raphy? You're awake?' A voice in the black.

Her! Shykit. What to do? 'Longtime? Gimme your hand… here.' *Felt her take it. I clutched.* 'Ain't letting you go again. You ran my rig in a ditch?' Heard her laugh, say something, squeeze.

'I… er… I always said I'd give up on the Radlands once I managed to bring someone out alive. Can't let you go.'

'What you saying, Raphy? I got nowhere to go.'

'Maybe we could stay together, for a time, you know?' *Froi— How stupid can I get? She'll be gone if y' don't say it, Me'Me.* 'Need you, Longtime. Froikit – I can't be without you, you awkward rad-riddled glowbag.'

'Harken to y'self… What you saying, Raphy?'

On-the-spot time. 'Froikit, Longtime. Y' not going to make me actually say it, are y'? Like, so I love you. There – that alright?' *Making a person say that.*

'That's not just the radiation and the pills talking, is it?' She was clutching at me. Pitfire! That hurt – bed still felt like gravel.

***

'Raphy? You haven't asked about The Find?'

'Practically forgot about it. Koh, was it? Burying your little archaeologist's head in it, are you? Still got the samples?' Eyesight isn't all it's cracked up to be: it hurts. But she'd been looking pretty good for the past day or two – younger-ish. Less radded-out. Smile on her.

'Well, considering the bits and pieces I brought out, and the paps and vids, there are dat-cubes of some type; some techno gadgets; maybe a few gems and jewels, bars and coins of ancient times. Worth millions, tens of millions. It's information, Raphy – it's *Pre-Civ History.*'

'So why're you looking less than utterly enthralled?'

'I am enthrall—'

'You're not. You look like me when I'm desperate to get drunk, but it'd mean going in the Zipper and Buttons bar after dark. Too big a risk.'

I knew I was right. 'You think it's worth a fortune in the spendable stuff, as well as intrinsic value? But you can't face going back for it? Too risky, state we're in?'

She looked shefterish. 'Can't go back there.'

'There's a possibility I can help. I have a partner—'

'A what? You never...'

'Yes, I did. Maybe. I have, anyway. Don't look like that. He's a hrypsid called Keffy, here in Astyar. Just as pluggle-faced as all the others, and equally as morals-bound. I told you, I have a sort of home up here... always said I wouldn't go back if I ever managed to bring one woman out alive. Yes, yes, I know it sounds stupid, but I really did have a run of ill luck in that direction.'

'Not as bad as theirs.'

There wasn't much to answer that with. It was true enough. 'This partner, Keffy, he has contacts that are spot-on honest. He can appoint a crew to do all the salvage. We've done it before with a couple of places I found.'

'And do what with it? It's Adrom planetary heritage. Central gov'll claim it. Or the universities?'

'Not a chance – they can't change their stance now. Relics have come our the Radiation Lands for decades. Nobody can claim cultural heritage – there's no registered official interest in the region. Me and Keffy are sanctioned prospectors, collectors and dealers – except I do the first two and he does the latter. Gov have first refusal; there's a list of institutions, private collectors and researchers next, on a competitive bid-offer.'

'But Vajan—'

‘Registered rights to the area and the finds. They probably didn’t tell you that. We have discretion to let some items go to less well-off bidders, to even things up. That works both ways – he can not accept bids, too. Unless Vajan is prepared to pay vastly over-the-odds in recompense, naturally. Otherwise, they don’t get a sniff at the planet’s greatest archaeological find yet. They’ll pay; he’s very good at this. He moves all my stones and relics. We’re partners – *sedulur*, as they say. They take such relationships very seriously.’

She was giving me a few cross-eyed looks.

‘We’d be more than wealthy, Fifty-fifty – after Keffy’s cut and expenses.’

She looked mightily pleased at the prospect.

‘I thought you were the academic type – the self-sacrificing knowledge-is-all worm?’

‘I was. Till they screwed us over the radiation poisoning, and the miserly pay-out over what we found in the Glowlands, and dad’s dismissal for arguing. Between them, they finished him. Yes,’ she smiled in a kind of smug satisfaction, ‘I’m sure I’d enjoy being rich, especially at their expense.’

‘Best not count on it, Longtime. I’m already more than wealthy, and do I look happy? Do I chufferty.’

‘You? Wealthy?’

‘You don’t have to look so disbelieving. My rig’s worth a hundred-thou – or it was till I let you drive. *Ah ah!* You can’t hit a poorly man. I have a home on the north coast – Roinstree Point. I should go there more often.’

‘Roinstree? I’ve heard of that. It’s—

‘I know what it is. I started putting my earnings into property after I was robbed of my cash and gems one time. Ain't nobody going to steal my home – except the sea, maybe, in a hundred thousand yonks.'

'It's where the Presidential Maenor is. You close to that, are you?'

'In a way…'

'What? It's yours? I don't believe it… But why? A place like that?'

'It was a derelict farmhouse in a terrible mess back then. Group of us looking for artefacts among the collapsing walls and rubble. One of the group was laughing that I was falling in love with the place – clifftop position, fine views, own beaches. I thought, "He's right." And I bought it, did up a couple of rooms and carried on collecting there, prospecting elsewhere. Did a few engine jobs when they needed someone stupid.

'So you? Built it?'

'Some of it, personally. Or paid for it. I thought if Corrianne came back with the kids… But I heard years ago she'd married. Oh, I didn't tell you she did another flier, did I? She's moved off Nowhere and froiked off in the direction of WhoCaresWhere with someone new.' *She couldn't stand the sight of me, with a head splurted and burned like this. And decided something similar about her merchant feller.'*

'So why keep Roinstree…?'

'I didn't mention the cellars, did I? How deep they are? How ancient? How relic-filled? It was quite a feat, drip-dropping a few items onto the market now and again.'

She didn't look too believing.

'Koh, so I keep the place. I still love the site, the views along the cliffs and beaches. Thought maybe I might bring somebody there. I dunno – been waiting for… you… maybe? I suppose…?' *I forget things. Like where I was when that accident occurred. What really happened to our vehicles.*

'Roinstree?' Longtime was struggling to believe it. 'The beach, palmettas, white sand? Turquoise sea? Oh, froik. If you're asking, the answer's yes.'

'I come with it, I'm afraid…' *Seeing them again, bogged down under that overhang. How it had all come back. I could have done the inventory there and then. Yorter! How it had flooded back.*

She laughed – lightly, eyes-twinkly, 'Have you ever actually lived there?'

'On and off. Building, recovering from one thing after another. Attempting to rebuild memories.' *Securing the cellars, sorting through the contents. Dripping hints onto the academic and collecting scene. Finding hints in the cellars' contents about where some of it had originated; planning an expedition out there.*

'Rebuild what?'

'My memory isn't real. I've had two serious head injuries, I think. One or the other really did for me. Can't recall. There was the rig that sank in the melt pond; and an eruption somewhere. Couldn't remember much after that – our collecting location, what I was doing, my real name. I had no recollection of Roinstree for several years – until someone recognised me.'

She was coming to sit next to me on the bed, 'No real memories?' Dubious? Incredulous, more like.

'Patchy. With old ones, I'm fine. The more recent ones I've re-built from flickers that come and go, the briefest of images or words. So I try to string them into a sequence that makes sense. I'm present tense only, as they say.'

'Your name? Is that real?

‘Raphaello? Sure is. My born name. Course, when a group of avvies found me, I was pretty bad: head.. lungs… lot of burns. Couldn’t speak. They called me Prospero; it means Fortunate in avvie. Like I was lucky to survive. Prospero *Sourman* – that means Silent One in avvie. So that was me for a time – prospecting, dealing, engine testing, escort, guide. Then a party of hrypsids from up here recognised me. Convinced me I was from Astyar… and Roinstree.

‘Of course, the hrypsids always make a hash of pronouncing Prospero Sourman. Prahfessa Samman, indeed.’

‘You’re jesting me. Prahfessa Samman? Professor Salmon? You?’

‘Something got lost in translation, I guess.’

‘You bastard! All this time out there!’ Talk about wild of eye. And backhand.

‘No. “All this time” is today; the past hour, maybe two. It’s sparking things off. My head’s buzzing, putting things together, filling in… I have to live for the here and now. Or maybe I could settle now, for a Longtime.’ She caught the jest on her name, and laughed, rather weakly. ‘And there’re some things in the cellars you might like to see.’

--- oOo ---

RIGGED AND READY

There's a ship lies rigged and ready up in orbit.

She's vast. The size of a village, the shape of a tangled tube with knobs and antenna all over it, thrusters, comms dishes, and one tiny, but mightily-powered drive unit somewhere near its centre of mass.

Today, the Spirit of Kolonia will set flight. Heading for New Pleasley, 137 light years away. A three-year journey for a colony ship. Then all that struggle and reward of creating a new living planet. Wonderful new lives for all those aboard. Except a bare minimum crew who would return the ship here when the colony was established and stable.

We've come to look around the outbound port, and then to see her off. It's been a long day, and a busy one: it's been years since we were last here, seeing a ship off. Some things we remember so clearly, others have changed. It doesn't seems so bright here now. Not so clean and shining. 'Maybe it was a good time in '54. Not enough time and cash for a brush-up nowadays?'

We stood at the panam windows in the private lounge – private for we repeat offenders, as they jest. A drink or two while we waited along with a few other couples. Yes, the lounge isn't its previously pristine self.

**

She rose at last, the Spirit, silently easy away from her grapple-berth. She performed a single full turn, slightly twisting. Precising herself in the specific direction for New Pleasley, 137 light years away.

A tinge of sadness as we watched, our five children aboard, partnered-up with same-age youngsters for marriage partnerships. They'd do well. We'd brought them up well over the past twenty-four years – resilient and resourceful, intelligent and hard-working. They would love their new lives.

Poised… any second now… A static flash, and the Spirit disappeared.

'That's it.' Mitri said. 'We're on our own again.' She turned away from the black-view window. 'Four generations of children we've sent into the Universe now.'

'Okay,' I almost slumped. It was always a wrench, letting your family go. 'We going to have a few drinks tonight? A few days resting up around here?'

'Naturally; we're entitled. Shall we start on the replacements tonight?'

THE FACILITY

Still well pre-dawn and I'm driving up Skillington Hill, out the village and out the lit-up area into the dark and mist towards the moors. I'm irritated more than a mite, still chuntering about Annabel and her 'Don't bother coming back,' as I'm shutting the door. But I need to be up Hindlow Peak before dawn, for the pics. It's a commission, so I've got to be out early. Like I'm rehearsing what to tell her when I get back.

Hadn't gone more than a mile and there's lights ahead, amber and flashing. 'What the chuff now? Like I'm not in a bad enough mood already without a delay getting up there before sun-up.' But I'm slowing down, drop a gear. Lights are red and blue now. Police? I'm thinking. I'm also thinking, Shuggeration. I don't need this on top of a bellyful of Annabel and the kids. So I'm coming to a cautious halt. Too narrow to U-turn and find another way. Have to see what's up. At least I haven't been drinking, and I'm taxed. 'Come on, Fuzz,' I'm chuntering to myself as I pull the handbrake on and look for who's coming out the misty light-glare. 'Lock me up. You look after four mouths and three backsides. At least Annabel manages that on her own.'

They don't look much like police, but it's misty and dark and glary-lit and they're in hi-vis and carrying batons. Must be cross – pulling overnight duty up here. One to each side of the car. Wind the window down. Ugly-looking copper. No uniform. Black bomber jacket.

'Somebody escaped from Hentonworth?' I'm asking. 'It's not me. I only escaped from my missus.'

Chufferty! It's not a baton that's swinging into view – it's twin circles. On the end of a double-barrelled shotgun. Chuffit. Just what I need. Mistaken for some escaped jailbird. Probably a mass murderer – except Hentonworth is for minor non-violent offenders.

'Get out the car.'

Great. A pair of robbing scousers. That accent doesn't come much stronger. 'Come on. Out. Now.'

Scared? Yeah, a bit, I suppose, but if I can survive one of Annabel's shrieky hissy fits, I can get through this. Goodbye to my cameras, though. Insurance should cover it. Maybe. So I'm carefully undoing my seatbelt, 'Hands empty, see.' I show them. Unlatch the door, climb out slowly.

'Stand over dare. On de vairge. Get yer hands up.' Oh Lord – that accent. There was a bit of a drop behind me from the verge into a field or something equally obscure. Maybe I could leap backwards down there and vanish into the darkness.

One of them had his torch in my face, and there was another going through the car… two others. Jabbering at me in that God-awful accent. My camera gear being ripped open and chucked all over the road and the grass. 'It's not here.'

'It must be.'

'Something I can help you with?' I offered. 'What are you after?'

'Shut de fuck up, yeww.'

'Charming.' To be honest, I was pissed with them more than anything.

He comes up to me, staring right in my face. I thought he was going to spit in my face, or give me a belt in the stomach.

'It ain't him, Yosser,' comes this voice from the back of my estate.

'Wha?' How the hell can you talk from halfway down your throat? 'Got to be.'

They all came round me, staring at me like it was my fault, and I'm thinking Come on, send me on my way, or clear off yourselves and let me collect my gear together. But it was obviously a big decision for them, not something they were accustomed to. I was really patient, keeping my hands up at shoulder height, and the one called Yosser with the gun called me a stupid bastard. *Me!* And it's *him* without whatever he came looking for.

And I saw his fingers clocking round the triggers, 'Shi—' Big flash and I'm hurtling backwards down the embankment. *He's shot me.* I'm rolling down all over the place. *What a stupid way to...*

Lying in cold wet grass thinking I can't still be alive...

Except it's not the grass, I'm on a bed. I'm still here. Don't believe it. Hurt. Aching all over. Chest feels bad... Long time. Dull light.

Them hijackers, whatever... Shot me. Couldn't possibly live through that. I saw the blast. Both barrels. In my chest. From three feet away. No way I'm alive.

There's a sheet on me. Scrubby rough cover. I can feel over it. I can move! I'm dead. A ghost. Must be the morgue or whatever they call body places. No, they'd have my face covered. Unless somebody's coming to view me?

Can't be heaven. Not like this. I've been cheated – it should be sunny and warm and friendly.

Eyes flicking open. I'm in a room. Heaven's a dingy place, I think. Nothing's moving. Looking without moving. It's a panelled ceiling. A plain pale almandine wall… the other way, a big window with curtains. Can't see through it. Trying to see behind me on the wall – lights, not on, a monitoring bank like they hitch patients up to. Except I'm not attached. Oh – something on my finger – plastic clip-on thing. Measure pulse or oxygen? What for? I mustn't be dead. I pull it off. Something starts beeping. Shuffle. It's slipped away… feeling round for it. Ahh, fingers a bit stiff, get it back on. The beeping stops. Good – irritating thing.

Between the taxman and the NHS, they've made a profit on me, alright. Not a day's illness in my life, even that Chinese flu. And the damn taxes I paid. Might get my money back on this.

There's a nurse looming over me, fiddling about. They have nurses in heaven? What for? We're all supposed to be well in heaven, aren't we? She's poking at the wall unit. Then pulling my covers straight.

'Hello,' I said.

'Ahh…ahh… ah… what?' she said.

I repeated it – can't have been so unusual, just, 'Hello'.

'You're awake.'

'Talking in my sleep.' I can be quick like that, sometimes.

She fiddled about more, asked how I was feeling, jotted something on a clipboard, shushed me and went.

I thought somebody would come and look at me. Tell me what happened. But nothing, and I was drifting off.

Brighter lights. Some people round. Annabel? Can't see her. Trying to check me over. I've been feeling at my chest – doesn't feel right – all lumpy and uneven. They're moving me and asking if I'm okay with sitting up a little, and I'm trying to help but they stop me, 'We'll do it.'

And I'm thinking, 'Jennifer, Alison, Annabel, too.' Me and her used to sing that one. 'Annabel? My wife? She coming soon?'

They didn't say.

'Where is this?' They stayed quiet.

'Am I alive?' No answer to that, either.

The lights were brightening up, curtains being pulled open. I was definitely in bed. Two nurse-types were pulling and heaving at me, sitting me up, heap of pillows shoved in behind me.

They motioned to the viewing window, *Annabel?* I thought. No. Two men were out there in a side room. They got nods from my nursey-types, and came in, gowns on. With a couple of big men first. Like an escort pair who stepped aside and stood there, blank-faced. 'Dangerous, am I?' I asked. They didn't even smile, just watched while two doc-types sat down to give me The Talk.

'Mr Malloy. Your DNA is totally unlike any other on record. Normally four natural building blocks make up all life's DNA and RNA. These form your genetic code. In laboratories, four more have been created, making the eight blocks of the hachimoji sequences. You have eight DNA blocks, and five of them are different again.' The one doing the talking paused and looked at me like it should mean something to me.

'So? What are you saying?'

The other one thought he could explain better. 'You're an alien.'

'Not from this planet—'

'Either that, or you're complete sport—'

'A freak, mutation on an impossible scale.' Number One was back in the fray.

'Bollocks, I'm as normal as you. I have two children… no, three – baby three weeks ago.'

They looked at each other.

'What?' But they wouldn't answer.

'Where do you come from, Mr Malloy?' And they kept on about it, just wanting me to tell them where I was from and what the planetary Zog was I up to. 'Where were you born? What are your earliest memories?'

They were going on about DNA like I knew all about double helixes and nuclear tides and nitrogens. Totally beyond me. And they still wouldn't say anything about Annabel. Or my children. Or what happened to me. 'Where am I? What is this place?'

'This is The Facility.'

'You trying to be enigmatic, huh? What happened to me? That feller shot me. I saw. Both barrels lit up and I'm flying back and dead.'

Another sneaky look at each other and they folded up their documents and left.

One of the heavies went with them. The other stayed with the nurse.

'Big mystery, is it?' I asked her when she brought me a cuppa and a syringe.

'You are,' she said, and smiled a tiny bit.

'What is this place?' While she's in a good mood.

'Not allowed to say. Government hospital for special cases,' she murmured as she leaned over and flashed a cleavage and put another pillow behind my head. 'Hampton.'

'Where's that?'

But she just smiled again. 'You've sure got them wondering. Alien, are you? Where from?'

'Hampton,' I piped back. 'Not allowed to tell you.'

Quite a nice laugh. But she departed with a hip flourish when she finished with the extraction of blood, the checking of bleeping electronics and taking of notes.

So I'm left sitting-lying here. And I'm trying to get my head round it… Me? An alien? They're taking the Mick.

Thinking back, when I was a kid… The biggest thing to happen to me and my sister Khariin, was when we fell in the lock in the canal. Trying to get away from a gang of big lads who were trying to rob us. I don't know where that was. I was thrashing in the water for ages – great high walls all round me. The lock gate all slimy and slippy. Clutching at a chain. Didn't see Khariin at all after we'd crashed into the water. Like she'd vanished.

I was so cold and shaking and wasn't going to be holding on much longer. Never knew who actually got me out. I remember I was in a hospital. 'For ages,' they said. 'You've been unconscious for two weeks.'

'Khariin?' They were blank. 'My sister?'

They never found her, even when they drained the lock and I knew she had to be there and I cried and cried and wanted her and they never found her. Or even where I was from, and I only knew my name, Eirien.

'You're imagining her.'

'Brain damage.' I hear them saying.

'Your name sounds Irish; not your accent, though.'

There had been gypsies moving through, for a big horse and pony fete and they thought I might be one of theirs. 'We're getting little cooperation from the travellers,' a policeman said. 'They're usually very protective of their children, and would surely have been glad not to have lost one. But they swear not.'

Six months of supposed enquiries came up with nothing about me or Khariin. By then I was in a home and somebody made an offer to foster me. 'He looks so sweet,' they said. Really nice, they were, actually, the Malloys. I had four sisters who'd been pestering for a brother. So that was me – fully adopted after six more months.

My memories dwindled to faint dreams after a bit – Sister Khariin. I remembered us laughing and plotting our plans and climbing trees and eating fabulous things… and it was all fading. My new sisters were just like Khariin in lots of ways – and we played together and looked after each other and went to school together and I was like a peacemaker with them sometimes. And defender – I didn't let big lads bully me ever again, like they had with me and Khariin. I used to think of myself as bigger than all of them put together, and I'd roar at them. I bet I looked really silly doing that – the littlest boy in the class. But we didn't get any bother.

Thinking about it now, I remember in that hospital, after being rescued from the water, I was having headaches, flashes of demon-like red faces. I saw some like it in a horror comic years afterwards, and it was really scary. I don't think of such things. I used to get nightmares. It was how I thought Hell must be when they said about it in school – shrieking, red and flickering. I painted it in art one time and it scared me and I ripped it up before the teacher saw it.

So now – another hospital. The first one I've been in since then. Interesting, but worrying. I shouldn't be in here. After a few days, I'm feeling alright, but they keep insisting I stay and won't answer questions and I was too weak and mixed-up to do much about it. They wheeled me into different rooms and always said it was up to someone else to tell me things. 'I'm only here to do my job… this particular test.' They all said the same thing.

So it was a constant round being wired up to equipment in different rooms, and inside scanners, or having them massage me all over – really intrusive they were. Were indignant when I wouldn't masturbate in a bottle for them, 'Bring me a neat little blonde,' I told them, 'and I'll see what I can do.' So they didn't get a sample of that. 'You could have done all that before, if I was truly unconscious for so long.'

A wheelchair at first, then a frame, then walking sticks.

And they talked at me incessantly… 'And before that? Your first sister? The girl called… Khariin?' I struggled and strained in my head, as I hadn't for twenty or more years. But I was dosed up on something and couldn't stay awake half the time.

> Faces… eyes so big, then closing to slits above hawklike beaks with long slitted nostrils… Creatures that chittered and yagged, excited… frightening at first… then laughing, so loud and deep…

I awoke, or was awakened by a nurse touching me, '…to talk to you, Mr Malloy.' A man in a blue-stripe suit. Always an ominous sign. Wanting to go through my past yet again, 'There might be something new that's been sparked, Eirien.' I didn't like him using my personal name. It's okay for the nurses – we're on intimate terms, one way or another. But I was hardly going to tell him about my dreams, was I? I was having them more. Maybe roused from their incessant yappering and probing.

> Faces looming of a sudden, all around me, yackering mouths like beaks. Red-gleaming eyes. Bony long fingers pointing and poking…

'And how do you feel about swimming? And flying?'

‘Oh? What? You think I’m an alien fish? Or bird?’

He shrugged in that really irritating some sneery people have. ‘We don’t know what you are, but your HNP – as we call it – like DNA – has piscine and avian gene structures – very similar to fish and birds—’

> Those faces again, great heavy beaks separating eyes that widened and slitted rhythmically. Angry, perhaps fearful. Fleeing, chased... a sense of panic. Red light beams flashed across and through them, criss-crossing.

I shivered. Those red beams held so much menace and power.

He tried to put the pressure on, almost threatening me, and I said he should leave me alone, let me go, not keep taking samples of me. He had this faint superior smirk, ‘In here, I can do whatever I wish.’

‘I feel like you already have. Kidnapped me, have you?’

That cold smile again. ‘We’ve taken good care of you. You were found twenty feet down a roadside embankment. Your car was burned out close by. You had almost no chest. Massive injury. But you weren’t dead. Still warm – without a heart, lungs and half your stomach.’

This wasn’t going in. ‘How then…? I couldn’t have… It’s impossible.’

‘Of course it is. But you did live. The ambulance took you to the hospital for certification of death – but you were still warm that afternoon and they kept you on a trolley. Two days later, my colleagues became aware, and we took you over. No rigor mortis, no heart or lungs to speak of; no further blood loss.’ He had the most icy smile I’ve ever seen. ‘So you must be non-human. Thus alien, by definition. There were signs of arteries re-forming, healing of the trauma sites, bones re-growing. My colleagues pumped you full of saline solution, whole blood, vitamins and everything else they could think of. Quite the little celebrity you were, in some circles.

'I don't believe it.' It was stupid. 'I'm normal. Not alien.'

'Explain how you had grown an embryonic heart within four days, then. Much like that of a foetus – which has a number of similarities with fish-foetus development. I tell you – you've had more scans, X-rays and the like than anyone else still alive. Not my area of expertise, though.'

'What are you, then?'

'DNA consultant, or HPA in your case. Whole new branch of knowledge and research, you are. The nearest I've encountered is a laboratory in the USA, which postulates the possibility of two of your genetic blocks being a viable basic for an alien structure.'

'You're losing me.'

'They had already theorised that kaolamine and decetamin could form the necessary nucleotide bonds, but only under certain very specific conditions.'

'You're sharing info on me? Isn't that a breach of—'

He shrugged, 'Information, samples of blood, muscle, bone tissue... There are pieces and samples of you scattered around the world. Leaps and strides, we're taking. This's Hampton. We need no permission for anything in here. Officially, you died six months ago on Skillington Hill – and were cremated two weeks later. You have no rights.'

'But, Annabel? My children?'

'Attended your funeral. Along with your adoptive parents, and two of your sisters...' He checked his notes. 'Steffi and Sarah.'

'Kate and Andrea live in Bali.'

'Indeed so. You, however, were in classified units in Sheffield and Manchester under a Jon Smythe ID, before coming here. You were far beyond critical – well off the survivable scale.'

'Yeah, okay, I'm getting that…' There was something here that didn't add up. They were right about that. Okay, change tack. 'What about the men who shot me?'

'Mmm, yes… There is a police report.'

'Wassit say?' I was flooding with apparitions of them – four of them – in the headlights and emergency lights up on the hill road. Misty, dark. Lousy thieving low-life gits. Shit – it was making my blood boil just to think of it – sneering face – twin barrels prodding me. In my face… in my chest…

> A howling face, mouth so broad, extending in a huge powerful beak, so wide. It opened, roaring… Fingers like daggers, so red, blood red and sharp. Lights flashing in brilliant crimson beams, illuminating all in gleams and flickers of fire.

I shivered. Immersed in the vision. 'What?'

Blue-stripe was open-mouth staring at me. He tried to speak. Something had upset him. Couldn't get the words out. Just, 'I'll review the police conclusions. Let you know.' He scuttled out. I didn't think he'd be straight back.

He wasn't.

It gave me time to think on it – that demon howling face – faces. Clutching hands with long, clawed fingers that reached… and reached so far. So powerful. Such *strength*. Something was stirring in me… hot like a fire flickering in my chest; aching, as if the fingers were clawing inside me, twisting and grasping. So frightening— the faces again – demonic, wide-eyed, then slitting. Beaks that ravened wide and snapped shut like bones breaking.

Alongside me, as though shepherding me. But… the warmth was not from the flames that wraithed around them, or the flashing beams… it was increasingly from within me, a cuddling warmth, a murmuring, hugging.

Lord, I ached, everywhere, in my bones. I stared at my fingers as though they were guilty – but no – they were the same as always, normal.

My chest… pulling my shirt open. Such a mess. Still a mass of lumpy scar tissue, but so much improved these past weeks. No hair yet, but I had nipples. *They're new.* And I could feel my heart throbbing. Tried to tell if it felt the same as it used to. *Who knows?*

Blue-stripe was back. With the usual two heavies plus a couple of new ones. 'I have arranged for new accommodation for you.'

'What?'

'More secure than here.'

'You want more secure than this?' I was eyeing up the heavies as they shuffled to outflank me. 'I don't think so. I want out of here altogether. You were going to tell me about the men who stopped me on the road.'

'The police report? Yes… here. So little to it.' He was dismissive, wafted a sheaf of papers round. 'They traced the assailants almost at once. Liverpool drug dealers attempting to waylay a rival's consignment.'

'So how come they got it wrong?'

'Who knows? Badly tipped off? Wrong info on the route? Wrong timing?' He shrugged, leafing through his papers, ignoring my staring demand.

'They were arrested then? Identified?'

'Identified, yes. Fingerprints were everywhere on your car… the bonnet, wings, where they pushed it backwards over the edge.'

'And my car, my cameras?'

'Forget them. Your wife collected the insurance months ago.'

'But… the men? You got them?'

'Me? I don't undertake the apprehension of villains. We requested that the police not follow-up. It wouldn't be in the national interest, you know.'

'Not what? Why?'

'National interest, I told you. You have alien DNA – HPN. That's far more important than attracting unwanted attention to our little project, or catching a few petty criminals. You are new. Very Different. You could be from another planet or from a visiting spaceship, for all we know.'

'Petty? Attempted murderers. Drug gangers? Armed robbers? They tried to kill me.'

He shrugged, 'They didn't succeed. No harm done.'

'No harm? I'm blown apart, lost my wife and kids, and six months out my life—'

'And we got an alien. You're worth your weight in platinum. And we're not going to lose you.'

> The faces are back, so real, all around me. Angered, reddened and howling-mouthed. Such strength in them. Such might. Enveloping me.

Their rage is building up in me, too. 'Tell me their names,' I demand of my shrugging jailor. 'These thieving scousers.'

'That's a police matter. It's been dealt with. It's of no further concern to us, or to you.' His menacing tone and stare are hardly going to freeze my Baldricks, now are they? The heavies are flexing their fingers, fists and shoulders.

'Their names,' I demand, getting to my feet, suddenly strong.

He attempts to rise… struggling to do so. Sat down again. His heavies are shuffling back. I'm towering higher, like I used to pretend when I was a kid. So powerful now. Stretching my mind and body, pushing upwards at the ceiling. It's bursting apart, and I tear it down with red-clawed hands. I howled down at the fivesome as they cower on the floor among the debris.

'Names.' I repeat, the brilliant galia beams flashing from my clenched hands, threatening the cringing creatures. I glower down upon them. Impatient, I demand again, the whole room glowing redly as the walls crumble and the adjacent rooms collapse in rubble. 'Liverpool, then.' That sparked anew in my mind – their scouse accents – so distinctly Liverpudlian. 'Yes, Liverpool.'

I look around, deciding… becoming terribly focused. I grow. Higher; so powerful. I grow tall beyond the building, and I look down over the spreading reddened rubble of buildings and high fences.

Liverpool? I gaze afar, orient myself. *That way – north-west.* Tiny below me, I see them cringing still, half-buried beneath ceiling panels and roof beams. I seethe down upon them and turn toward the north-west.

'Cross Liverpool off your maps.'

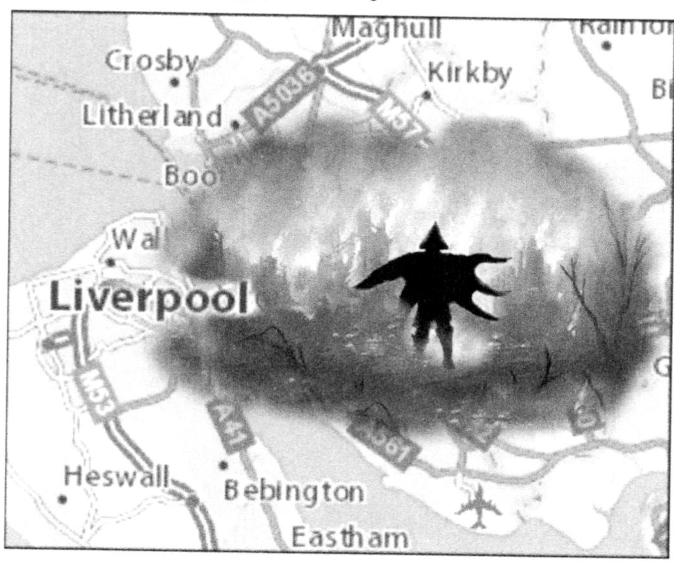

THEY CALL THE WIND PARIAH

'Zaimie, you need to stay in during the evenings.'

It's not fair. Daddy never lets us play with the other children in their dome houses or in their yards, or on the avenues and the park.

'But Daddy,' I say, 'I'm seven. Everybody else my age plays out with their friends. And I go to school and the shops, the leisure centre and the community hall and the sports stadium.'

'Zaimie, I know it's difficult at your age, but this is a dangerous planet – full of all manner of infections and diseases. We need to keep them away, and not go out after dark, when they are at their worst.'

*

'My little Zaimie just doesn't understand the risks of being out after dark,' I told Gorj at the Scion Atmosphere Plant where I work. 'She doesn't realise that some of the native wildlife has been known to come into the village, and you know how vicious the Codropads can be with their pincered tentacles. And there have been reports of them causing infections through their bites and nips.'

'I thought you did it because the yards at night are full of insects and diseases rising off the river?'

'Yes, that is the main reason, but she can't picture that, like she can with animals. I've been reading and watching all about it on Central Enviro Channel. Terrible statistics on deaths, and what's lurking in the outer lands. This's still a new colony, you know. We haven't conquered everything on Recension in the past thirty-odd years.'

*

'My oppo at work, Nash – yes, him with the little blonde girl, Zaimie – he never listens to any sense. He always knows best. Whenever I tell him that he'll never become naturalised to the environment if they're never exposed to it, he's got an answer. "Your children will never learn to cope with dangers, or diseases," I say. "Or learn to be sociable, Nash. You need to let them take chances, get used to the environment. All of it, not just the daylight hours."

'I've been on at him several times, but he goes on about surviving, reckoning that when the next cuckust swarm descends on Wheel Village, and we all get bitten and come down with the skin-rot, then he and his family will be laughing at us and they'll be safe in their dome.' Gorj paused while Annie nodded very sagely and mumbled something about, 'They weren't very neighbourly, were they?'

'I'm right, aren't I, Annie? They need to get out; poor kids won't know how to play together; and they'll catch every summer sniffle that's going round.'

'Yes, dear. I quite agree, but what can we do about it?'

'I wondered if you might have a word with Abcynth? She's on the school committee, isn't she?'

*

'Abcynth? Your little girl goes to the community school, doesn't she? My Gorj was telling me about Nash and the way he keeps all his family in their dome all night, every night. Do you know her? Little blonde girl?'

'Yes, my Kathy knows her from school. Ah – she's here now.' Abcynth turned as the dome door slid open. 'You know Zaimie, don't you dear?'

'Yes, she's in my class, but she often doesn't come in if there's a wet nose or diarrhoea going round. She's nice.

But never plays with us. Don't think she knows how. Never shares her sweets, either. She says her daddy's scared that one of the roaming bands will kidnap her out their yard, for sale on the novelty slave market. She's good at maths and languages, but she does a lot from her own dome, and her daddy tells them they'll be the only ones left alive if the river fever comes to Wheel Village.'

'Or if a fire sweeps through the educentre; or if everybody there catches the deformity sickness. "We'll be the only ones left, you see." That's what he tells all his children.' Kathy smiled sweetly up at her mum and Mrs Annie, more keen on finding out what was for tea than talking about some girl at school who they didn't see very often, anyway.

'Zaimie said her daddy told her about a commune up north that was laid up for days on end when the dust mites got into their food. And it's not going to happen to them.'

'I wonder if you could go and see her when she's next in school, Kathy? Perhaps ask if you can play in their yard, or do your schoolwork at her dome?'

'She once told me that it stays sealed all the time, and nobody goes in.'

'Ask her if she wants to join your friend group for one of the study evenings. I bet Maxil's mum would happily deliver everyone back home after.'

'Or we stay at each other's places sometimes.'

*

'Mummy? Zaimie-next-door hasn't been in school for nine days, and my teacher said, "Does anyone live near her?" and I said, "I do," and she said, "Can you go and see if she's alright?"'

'Yes, alright, Keith, dear. I bet they've heard about the fluella virus going round. It was on the news that someone in Yickstown caught it and they're in quarantine. Why don't you take your sister round with you? *Kathy!'* she yelled out the back door.

So me and sis got made to go round to Zaimie's dome home. I never liked her, nor her brothers, especially Heggerty. Not normal, they aren't. But there's no answer. And the heat sensor on their door is registering high. We tried the outer doors and they were locked inside. We couldn't hear the aircon working, and there was no sign of anyone in the back yard. They don't have any livestock or pets – not even a guard stogger or a few chickarees from the woods. Heggerty once told me they're scared the stoggers'll turn on them like that pack that went wild over at Langley Wheel.

I'm going to tell our teacher about it. It was her who made us go round. It isn't right to be locked in all the time.

*

When children come to me with their concerns, I listen and do what I need to. Keith and Kathy said that Zaimie's father often exaggerates how dangerous it is out in the open, and the nights. 'He's always telling them how horrible it is to mix with all us disease-ridden children and people in the leisure and educentre. That's just not nice.'

In this case, I got on the viddy and informed our welfare manager, Mr. Refah. We checked the records and decided we should both go round.

'You're right, Miz Athro,' he confirmed when we arrived at their dome. 'All locked up. Still no sign of life. This is worrying. They've surely not moved away?'

'Become total isolationists, perhaps,' I ventured?

He blipped Mr Johtaja, his co-manager, to come, so the two of them could formally seek entry, to check if all was well and still there.

'We'll unzilp the doors and call out; then go in, cautiously, in case they object to our entry,' he said. So we did.

*

'They're all dead. Every one. In bed or in the lounge. When you first called, I hadn't really thought things could be very serious, not in our little commune wheel. Certainly not like this. Fungus all over them.'

We resealed the dome and called in the decontamination squad from Mainton.

They were coming and going for two days. We all watched from a safe distance, and it was decided to burn down their dome completely. That seemed such a shame. And with their bodies inside, too. That was awful, especially smelling the smoke, like cooking plastic.

*

As Decon Supervisor, it was my decision to incinerate the dome, having sought counsel from Mrs Naddaff at Mainton Central PH Unit. 'There's a group of travelling fair people here,' I said. 'And there's quite a crowd in town for the Overday Market. We need to burn it all away before anyone tries looting the place – some of them have been eyeing the place up. And they travel on tomorrow.'

*

I concurred with Rena, the on-the-spot Decon Officer. 'Burn it down. Make sure you do it thoroughly, rather than risk some new fungus getting out, like at that Rickoh place last year.' Rickoh's all cleared up now, of course, but it was rather nasty at the time. Same as the river fever, it spreads, we get immune to it. I'll let the news people at Local ECNS know. I've talked with Wesney Jill before. She'll want to know about something of this nature for broadcasting.

*

'Yes, this is interesting, Mrs Naddaff,' Jill said. 'Real news for a change. Might indeed be lessons to be learned. We'll do a cast about this tragedy. Eight persons? Locked in together so long?'

'Yes,' I filled her in on a few details. 'The aircon never had a rest or proper cleanout, so the fungus built up, and became so virulent. I'll get some background together for you. Yes, it's very unusual for local diseases or wildlife to do anything worse than debilitate a few people for a few days – an octo or two at most.

'Ah, they had no immunity?'

*

My fellow Newscaster, Mork, came over to my desk. 'Hey, Wesney, I saw a report on the early broadcasts. This morning in Bluff Town, or was it Carrith Bottoms? Some folk had come down with a fungus.'

'Let's look.' Wesney Jill flipped the search-casts on. 'Yesss. Both places, actually. And that on the cast now looks like another. Where's that? Hawking? Long way from the other three.'

'I'll see if I can trace any link. Travellers or something like that.'

'And I'll contact Caryn Key in Central City. They'll probably want to give the initial Eyes-up Alert on a wider scale, just in case.'

*

'This is Central News On Line. It is now confirmed that the epidemic that has wiped out 90% of the population in the Southern Plains region originated in Wheel Village. Plans to isolate the whole continent are now complete, and will remain in force for the foreseeable future.' Caryn sagged despondently. 'Should this spread any wider, a ten percent survival rate would devastate the whole planet. With a million or more people killed, our economy would be in ruins. No-one would visit ever again. We would become a pariah planet.'

*

Across the broadcast desk, Chief Medical Officer Muller Kintyre, from Central Gee, was hopeful. 'I believe this unprecedented outbreak has been contained, although we re considering full emergency measures if no antidote is found. Our best efforts have so far been in vain.'

He coughed a couple of times. *Perhaps I shouldn't have paid that publicity visit to the facility yesterday? Just a summer sniffle, I expect. Still, can't put this off. I'm due to be interviewed on the ECNS Channel. Hmm, yesss. Right about now. The Midnight to Dawn show – the Gravedigger Shift, as they call it.*

*

'And it's welcome to Medical Officer Kintyre, who has all the latest info on this terrible epidemic. This is Marshall Howe speaking. Yes, yes, Muller, call me Gravedigger. Everyone else does when they come on air. Now: you have claimed that this shocking outbreak is contained, haven't you? But you have previously warned that fungus spores are extremely light and could have been carried by the winds to anywhere on the planet by now?'

Medical Officer Kintyre was silent, clearly pondering over his answer, so Gravedigger prompted a little further. 'You have said the fungus could spread without personal contact? On the winds?'

Kintyre coughed uncomfortably, 'Er, I… indeed so—'

'— and that to travel off-planet,' Gravedigger Howe butted in, anxious to get a clear answer, 'would be "inconsiderate to other worlds"?'

Kintyre's discomfort with the questions and his own health was clearly increasing.

'And yet,' Gravedigger Howe continued relentlessly, 'is it not also rumoured that several of your colleagues – senior government officials – have booked long vacations off-planet, for themselves and their families?' He paused for a reaction. None came from the Medical Officer, so he carried on regardless. 'Indeed, we have it on good authority that some government officials may already have left Recension. One was quoted as saying he was leaving, "Before the winds make this a pariah planet… cut off from the rest of humanity."

'However, Officer Kintyre, if the spores are, according to your previous statement, already around the whole of Recension, is it not highly likely that these government officers will be spreading the—? Are you alright, Sir? Do you need a drink? Careful, you'll cough your— *Urgh. Yuck.* Er, anyway…'

He quickly turned back to his broadcast. 'I have the feeling there's *so* much further to run on this story. So, as I always say, "Signing off for another night, and wishing you all well. This is Marshall Howe at Eyam Central News Service."'

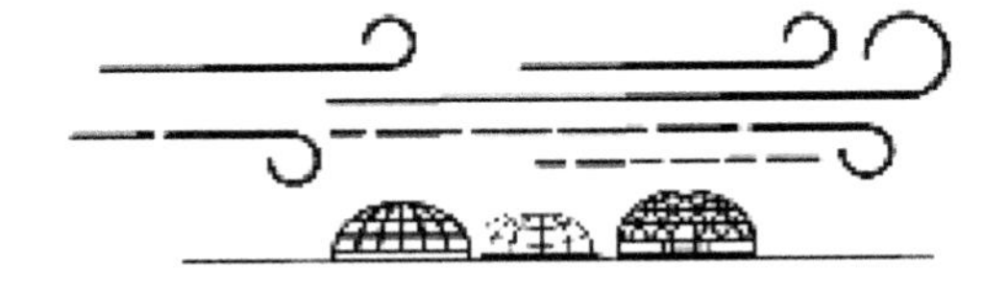

TIME OF THE GAP

It was moving. The impossible was occurring. King Tree was shaking. The ground around its mighty roots trembled. It creaked in ear-stabbing screeches. The air filled with the horrifying sound. piercing

We edged away, too afraid at the unbelievable happening. The whole forest – the World – echoed with the sound. 'King Tree is in agony,' Cayto whispered, afraid to be heard. 'This *cannot* happen.'

'It has the height of an hour-long walk…

'The strength of rock…

'The girth of our temple…

'It is King Tree…

'Yy-goth!' Again the ground shook. My feet thrust up by the sudden movement. Tossed backwards, we scrambled further away. Just in time. The ground burst between Jareth and me. The cracking sound of timber, as when a branch might fall, but more terrible. Close – here and now. Among us. Another upheaval. We clutched at the rough bark. A shattering sound from above. King Tree jerked. 'It moved. The Tree.' I gasped for breath.

Vastly high into the great great canopy, further than anyone had ever climbed, there was movement. Small branches crashed down around us. Moments later, leaves thudded close by, or fluttered away. We all scattered to shelter against other tree trunks, each of them a two-minin walk around the base.

We watched, our little forage group. Until now, it had been a good expedition – two slother-beasts that live in the greensky had fallen. 'Perhaps they were fighting,' Jareth said when we found their pulvered bodies.

‘Doesn’t matter,’ I said. ‘Get them wrapped. We’ll carry one home, and dine well this night, and return for the other tomorrow.’ *I* wore the uniform on that three-day expedition. My first time with the silver wings and flames. Symbols of power and right – the same as those inside The Shrine. So whatever I said was what was going to happen, and we carried the slother in teams.

It was a long way through the permanent shade of the forest. The unusually large amount of tree litter around this area had made progress exceedingly slow. ‘Something’s disturbed the sky,’ I said, and the others agreed as we clambered over fallen branches.

‘We saw the canopy waving more than usual yesterday. It even disturbed the stillness down here. Ah well, these’ll do us well for kindling.’

Branches falling? That happened on occasion, but for *this* to happen? A tree had never before trembled. Not a whole tree. *Not King Tree* – the fabric of the world.

Craaaack! A root thicker than a man sprang into the air, hurling Cayton and Jareth back amid a mass of flying soil and rocks. A shrieking splitting noise pierced our ears. The forest was changing.

‘King Tree is moving! It’s leaning!’ Cayton’s jaw quivered in disbelief. ‘It’s impossible – trees are for ever.’ More and more it leaned. Another root dragged and screamed upwards, finally wrenching into the air in a cascade of litter and rock. Slowly… slowly… a fearsome angle of threat and doom – King Tree moved away. Its mighty trunk leaning more and more. Klith and Matty ran – anticipating it coming even down to them. The world was ending in the greatest crashing sound imaginable. All around, the permanent fabric of the forest was turning on its side and over. *A tree is falling. Impossible – trees are for ever.*

Branches sundered and roared all around. Ear-splitting cracks had us down, cowering and clutching each other. A vast bough crashed and bounced not five paces from me. It shook and shuddered. As did I. Huge limbs of other trees were smashed apart by the power and vastness of the great one as it fell among them. Its base was lifting, tearing itself from the ground. Roots springing up.

'It's coming down…' The tones so hushed in awe at the dreadful thing. So close now – looming over, so colossal. It formed its own sky, so briefly in a mass of splintering crashing branches and leg-long needles and cones that thudded and shook the ground all about us in a maelstrom of fallingness. A great cacophony of sound and terror.

*

The ground heaved. It shuddered and trembled. Nearby trees were pushed aside by its enormous branches, and more branches fell in an endless rain of splintered timber and man-sized leaves. The mightiest noise the world could ever know. An impossible angle… raging through the other trees.

A tree is coming down. King Tree – the greatest of all. A mile high. An expedition was lost forever in its towering heights. Not even a single body had fallen.

It was down. The crashing was tremendous, the cloud of debris hurling back up among the branches. King Tree bounced. Once. Then shuddered. And settled. The rain of debris continued… leaves and cones, flowers. A creature with short striped fur. It twitched and sagged. 'Count our numbers.' All here as we re-gathered, shaken, but unharmed, other than the terror at the sight and sound of a tree falling – the Impossible. 'But the trees are the world,' we said.

'Look,' I stared up. We all stared. 'The canopy…'

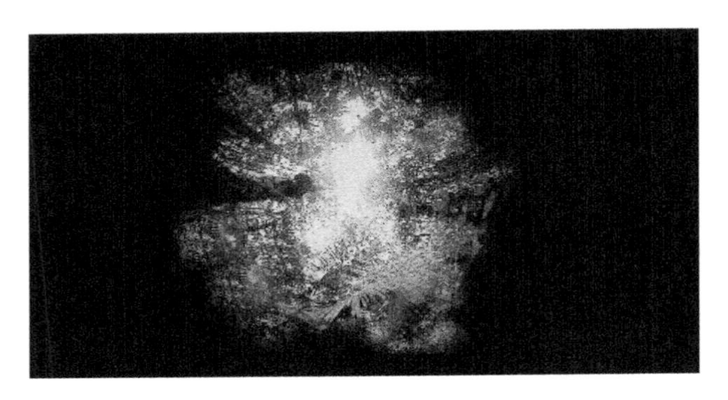

'The greensky... is split apart.' Aghast, we stared. A Gap in the Sky. Almost on my knees. 'It's destroyed.' The beautiful green and dark and dappled ceiling of the sky was shattered and broken – a raging gap – a dreadful brightness.

My eyes burned in the rays that struck down at us. Incredible columns of brilliance penetrating the trunks and branches. We looked. We saw the monster light that was eating the sky and had smashed King Tree down. Lying thirty steps away, a wall of earth and roots like an enormous spider with arms that reached for the canopy. Still it groaned, in the throes of death. Already settling into the ground and the undergrowth, the litter of leaves still drifting upon it.

We shrank back. 'What is this? Brilliance? Where is the all-promised Higher Sky of velvet blackness? The star points of light that we shall drift among, go back to, settle in?'

'Is it all lies? The Belief?' Jareth asked. 'We cannot have come from such eye-scorching radiance.'

'Have faith. Have faith,' I tried to reassure them. 'The World has not come apart. It's but one rent—'

'*One* rent? But it was *King Tree.* It is no more.'

'The start of how many more?' Klith demanded. 'Is it the first of many?'

We fled, escaping the reaching claws of light that brillianced our faces and stung our eyes. Away from the catastrophe; to hide and recover and return to the village – not two-dozen arrow-flights away.

*

Our leaders and elders were mouths agape. 'You actually witnessed such an event?' Non-plussed at our survival, they took us aside, 'We need every detail of what you recall, how you felt, what you actually saw.' As though it was a phenomenon to be studied, not a catastrophic blow to The Belief

A brief conference. We went to the Landing Ground, where stood The Shrine, the great gleaming smoothly metallic egg that brought our forebears here – or so The Belief would have it. Within, it held all knowledge. In its omniscience, would The Shrine have the wisdom now? *Can it help us in this time of fear and destruction?*

The elders talked and debated, and consulted the Shrine. For long minutes they tapped and asked, and checked on the keys and banks and screens.

'This is our opportunity to escape... to rejoin the stars...'

What? Do they intend to do battle with the great furnace above the sky? Does it really exist?

'Who will go?' they asked each other.

They speak of salvation and rescue? 'What is that?' I asked, utterly lost in the all-knowing words of the Elders. 'What imprisonment? You would leave here? To be eaten by the—?' I hardly knew what to call it. The fabled, the unseen. 'Does the fiery mouth truly glower down above the canopy?'

'The Gap is a window,' they said, 'to the Higher Sky. At present the fiery face dominates, and when it goes, the darkness comes. And through The Gap we shall see the starlight points.'

'We must be fast,' Elder Gor-captain said, 'for the surrounding trees will quickly cover the rent and seal it up.'

'We have perhaps a day or two. The forest does not like the light to penetrate to its soul. The leaves will spread, very swiftly. If the Gap is also to be a doorway, we must go through as soon as we may.'

*

I'm so afraid. The thought that The Belief could have hidden truth… as they say now. I took them to the place of the crashed remains of the most vast and ancient tree there'd ever been. It had truly happened. A part of the Sky had torn apart and come down to us. Up we gazed, and we waited and watched.

'See? See? The darkening… The starpoints.'

It was. The fabled Higher Sky with points of light, there to be seen by all who'd come. Where we could travel in the Shrine, and drift among the starpoints.

*

It's been decided – we're now three hundred strong, from forebears numbering twenty-eight, who came here in The Shrine. The leaders claim they can make The Shrine reach to the stars and take some of us out – to seek for others of our kind. To return and take all who wish to go. 'But only now,' they insist. 'We cannot wait for council meetings and The Belief Elders. It must be now. Tomorrow at latest.'

'The Shrine that is the egg of our origins can fly again; it can burst through The Gap before it closes. And it will fly again through the blackness to the stars whence our forebears came.

'Another day, possibly two, and The Gap will be gone – our green and dappled sky restored once more.'

*

They seek volunteers to enter the shrine, and accompany them, soaring through the high branches. But so few wish to leave. Too afraid to lose all they have here, where life is safe and constant. Six elders are willing. They seek two-dozen more.

Though sore afraid, and I know I'll be roasted and eaten by the blazing mouth, I'll go, and drift among the stars. And seek others of our kind.

There's nothing for me here.

Not since just before the forage expedition, when I was so proud of being invited to wear the uniform that I asked Kizi Orman to wed me.

And she turned me down again.

TOGETHER AGAIN

The action has taken its toll on us,
But there's a ship that's bound for Earth, they say,
So we all hold dreams of going there.
And it's certain we will, and soon, we pray,

Though what state we'll be in is anyone's guess.
We captured an enemy ship last year;
And they said, in that sleepy way when they're
Under the 'tathol, and filled with fear

That they intercepted our last ship back.
'No people aboard, just dross,' they swore.
'A cargo crate packed full of scraps
On a course that headed for Workshop Four.'

Not Earth itself? Some difference there:
Like a dozen light years, in the round.
That's six days plus in XL drive
For any ships that are Earthside bound.

No R&R ships for the likes of us.
Just broken bodies the enemy's killed,
Transistor minds and organ parts,
In a ship that waits till its banks are filled.

Pulped in mind and smashed in frame,
They're the likes of me and you, my friend.
They reckon Joe Fore is mostly Hayme,
With a hint of Cedric and Aramend.

I look around and it scares me stiff,
For I've seen Dean's arm on Harry Louth.
And something he said the other day
Came straight out of Nerky's mouth,

So Harry's not Harry inside his head.
The Pit alone knows what they do
With us, or how, or even where,
For the enemy's slaughtering every crew.

So why, oh why, are we fighting still?
Have we anyone left to wage this war?
Is everyone else just sitting around,
Cheering us on, and wanting more?

Through chips in our heads, they share with us
I'm certain that someone's prodding me,
For I feel the meddling probes within,
That forced me out on a reckless spree,

With tactics I'd never consider myself
When we raided their base near Aragorr.
I think I had three thumbs one time;
Though I never had boobs *and* balls before.

'We'll mend you fast; we'll ease your mind.'
But I never dreamed that they meant this,
The time they said, 'We'll soothe your pain,
And put you all together again.'

TYPICAL MAN

Anni glanced round the Tula Nest and Snack Bar, spotted her friend and slid into the empty seat to chat. 'How're your little ones these days, Tara?'

'Oh, still at the crawling stage. They'll be up and running round soon, I reckon. Little legs scuttling everywhere; antennae into everything that's not sealed and webbed down.'

'Still be under your feet, eh?' Anni utched her egg sacs up to ease the weight off her aching abdominals. She sighed and took a long sip at the rather divine drink on offer. 'We never seem to be free of'em, do we?'

'Mmm, what you were saying about your Rory – typical of a man, isn't it? All mandibles and no sense – that's mine all over, too.'

'Indeed, gobbo or what? I despair of him sometimes: he scarcely stops telling me how great he is, and when he does take a break, it's only to stuff himself with more food as fast as he can manage. The original big mouth, he is.'

'Ooh, really? Bit on the heavy side, is he?'

'Nearly squashed me the other week, he did. Never listens when I complain about it. Absolutely typical man, eh?' Tara let a few eyes drift over the selection of sweets available in the displays.

'Mine never listens to sense if it's coming from me. And I'm packed with wisdom.'

'Of course. Aren't we all? My Yorgie's gone completely deaf to sense – take the other day: there he was, him and this other man who I don't know. They were slurping a few jugs after work—'

'As they do.'

'Going on about us.' Tara eyed her drink up and wished she'd had a nut-bar crunch to go with it.

'The nerve. No, no. Don't tell me, Tara, I can't bear to hear – I can imagine. They're all the same when they get together over a drink.'

'You don't need to tell me that. I've had enough by the time he's gone out to work in the morning.'

'Me, too. Where's Yorgie work?'

'He's at Transit Corporation. Down the depot. He calls it *Handling*, but that's just Man-talk for looking after the consignments that come through.' Tara reached for another of the sweet juice drinks and took a long, sucking sip.

'Mmm? What sort of consignments?'

'He's in the aliens department, passengers in transit. He was telling me yesterday about this load they had coming through. Said they were alien as they could be – a species that comes in two different types, one of which is called the Man.'

'Yes? No? Same as us, are they?' Somewhat awed, this was new to Anni.

'Sort of, but not dead the same as us: their differences are bumps and protrusions and colourings. Not that he's seen any of them without their outer coverings, of course, but he's seen some pictures. He says there isn't actually much difference between them. Not as much as there is with us. Their differences are to do with how they reproduce, that's all.' Tara felt distinctly smug that she knew something that Anni didn't. 'They join together – they call it sex.'

'Ah, I've heard of that. Not clones or monos? But why would that matter if they're fairly small differences?

'I don't know, but he says the differences are only in which appendage of one fits in with the bits of the other one, like an interlink puzzle.' Bemused at the whole concept of other species being dimorphic merely because of their reproductive mechanism, Tara sucked on her juice drink. 'Purely for reproduction,' she repeated, glancing knowledgeably around the other sippers and munchers in the dining area.

'Well, if they're long-time travelling together, I hope they get on better than me and my Man at the moment.'

'Mmm, me, too. But it sounds like they're pretty similar to us in that way. Somebody told Yorgie the one known as the Man is always bossy and stupid.'

'Just like ours.'

'Only, with them it's purely because of these minor reproductive differences. Weird or what?'

'And they call their silly pushy one the Man, too, do they? Typical Man, isn't it? Same as ours – thinking they're so superior, just because we've got a proboscis, and they have a huge pair of Mandibles.'

ZERO 9-4

'Let me put this in words even a fourteen-year-old will understand, Natilie—'

'Daddy, I'm twelve. You even get your years mixed up. Christmas Day, twelve years ago, remember? I don't know how you manage with trilli-seconds...'

'Ahh, yes. But I thought if you stopped acting like a sixteen-year old, then we could average you out at about fourteen.'

'You invariably give me that funny look when I say things, Daddy. So how is your TTA supposed to work better if it tries to move you, instead of a gram of platinum and Harry?'

Daddy had that extra-patient look. He's very good at it.

'We tested it with units of one thousandths of a gram of gold first. Not a single unit moved in space or time. Not once. Not by a millimetre or one second. With recalculations , our theorists are now wondering if there might be a trigger amount – which we're calling Zero 9-4 – of the material for the time effect to take place.'

'Perhaps it went and came back within a single grain of time, Daddy?' I remember saying that to him when I was only eight. And I'm not so sure about it now. 'I mean, if physical matter can be in lumps called bosons and protons and things, why can't time be?'

'Because our best calculations say so,' he always said.

And I always told him, 'That's simply an excuse: if you can't explain it to a child then you don't really understand it yourself.'

'Do you understand the certainty of cause and effect, Tilly? Like arguing with your father and losing your spending money?'

I told him that was the coward's way out, and he said, 'Yes, but I'll be a rich coward, and calm with it. Whereas you'll be an impoverished hero.'

'Heroine,' I corrected him.

'Never mind heroine,' he told me. 'Stick with cocaine.' He always tried to joke his way out of a losing situation. Next, he'd ask what he'd done to deserve me and I'd say if he couldn't remember then I could give him a few hints.

He said that once when I tried to ask him about the calculations I'd been looking at, on the subject of time and dark matter, and there were certain similarities. 'Can you explain to me what those similarities indicate, Daddy?'

He never could. He looked a bit bothered, and said he'd look into it.

'So while you're looking into the similarities, can you look at the *differences* as well, please? I'm not clear about some of them myself, especially how you're so sure your value of Zero 9-4 is correct.'

Actually, I think he really was upset then, but I suppose he had a lot on his mind, being in charge of all those experiments with jumps in time. And nothing seemed to have worked for a long time.

'But even that one speck of platinum just sat there doing nothing. Then vanished. You didn't find out why or where, or when it had gone, even with an mf per second film.'

'That's it, Calamity Jane,' he told me. 'Tell me I'm a failure.' But he was laughing.

And I said, 'I'm Natilie Jane, not Calamity Jane. And it'll not be me who's the calamity if you haven't figured it out by the time you attempt to time-jump yourself. Look what happened to Harry.' Actually, we didn't know what happened to Harry.

'That bloody rabbit was there one trilth, and gone the next,' he said. I was there the day they did that. Daddy was everso good, letting me go in with him. 'And Harry never came back.' He was very upset that day. Not about Harry, though. And probably not as upset as Harry was... or will be, if he went forward in time.

'Perhaps we haven't got to the time when he does come back, Daddy,' I wondered. 'So where will he be now if he's going to turn up some time in the future? Will he be older? Or the same age as he is now? Or then?'

Daddy shrugged. 'Who knows? Maybe he'll be back on his carrots next week.'

'Or perhaps he's dining with dinosaurs right now.'

'That's it Tilly, be positive.'

'I do always try to be positive, Father. But you don't like me to ask questions.'

'I—'

'No, you don't. But, if I *am* allowed to ask, then why, if it's a time-space *continuum* – meaning they're aspects of the same phenomenon – then why do you assume that Harry travelled in time, not space?'

'What's that supposed to mean?'

'You don't need me to tell you that, Father. You know that the Earth's spinning around itself at a thousand miles an hour; and round the sun at seven thousand. And the sun is going round the galactic centre at eight million; as well as expanding into nothingness as the universe expands. So Harry could have popped out of your time bubble a billion miles away – where we were in the relative space-time continuum when he disappeared. Not where we are now – in a part of space-time that might not have existed when you pressed the button to send Harry away.'

'Ahh.' That was father's exasperated look. It usually comes on shortly before he sighs deeply and goes away muttering.

'And next, you're going to send yourself; and you're taking a red ping-pong ball to let go of when you arrive somewhere, so we'll know.'

'I'm quite sure I'll think of some way to return, Natilie, or let everyone know what happened.'

'From the Mid-Jurassic?' I asked him. 'You'll be eaten by dinosaurs.'

'There weren't any in this area.'

'*Here* was somewhere else then, Father. Trillions of zillions of miles away.'

'*Here* was in the tropics, Young Lady. Look at all the fossils of fern forest in the area… and the coral reef fossils the other side of the river.'

'That's not relative, Father. It's literal. And you've always told me that the Mid-Jurassic was a trillion-trillion miles and yonks away – hundreds of light years. The Earth wasn't here. I bet Harry popped up in the middle of space, where the Earth was 170 million years ago.'

'He can't have gone that far, timewise. There wasn't enough power going into the system to do that. It didn't reach Zero 9-4.'

'But you don't know that. You don't know what the trigger point is, in power level, or mass. It could just be a tiny bit more power being needed to spark a huge jump in the amount of mass being moved.' Daddy was being obb-dur-something that Mommy sometimes said. Silly-awkward. 'Can I ask one more question please? Thank you.' I didn't like that smile he put on when he teased me.

'When it didn't work with one thousandth of a gram of gold, you calculated how much power it would take to move it next time you tried. But you can't do that if you don't know how close you came to moving it. You might have—'

'Alright, I—'

'But you have no idea. It's not as if it trembled or got warm or looked like it was about to jump—'

'Tilly, please—'

'You can't just say it needs a thousand times more. It might be just twice as much. Or a million times more.'

'Natilie—' He had that look again.

'And you don't know how far it went in time, or space.'

'Yes, yes, alright. Tell me what you're getting at, Natilie Jane?'

'Perhaps…' I'd been puzzling about it a long time. 'Did the power go into the time? Or the space? Or the mass of what you were sending?'

'We're not exactly sure about that.'

'So if there's a certain mass sitting there, and a certain amount of power, what decides whether the mass goes a million miles, or a million years? Or… or… if half the mass goes two million?

'Come on, Till. Get to the point.'

'Well, next time, you're going to change two things – the mass – yourself instead of Harry. And ten times more power. That's not good science, Daddy.'

'Our calculations—'

'But, it could send a tenth of you ten million years back in time. Or forward.'

'Then you could be Happy Little Orphan Natilie, couldn't you?'

'I wouldn't be happy, Daddy. I love you everso much. And I wouldn't be an orphan because I would still have

Mom. And the tenth that went might be just your feet, I suppose. And most of you would still be here. So… how does the force decide how to balance mass and time and space and power? I find it very puzzling.'

'So do we, Young Lady. But not to worry: I took out a lot of extra insurance on all of us, as well as the company's indemnity.'

'So we're supposed to be unhappy about you, but pleased with some extra money? Suppose—' it just occurred to me, 'you said the force is more efficient when it gets about the trigger level of power and mass? So what if the force decided that the mass was the whole of you… and the bubble chamber… and the laboratory… *and* the whole of MIT… *and* all of Boston? And sent you all one year back or forward? Or a mile up in the sky?'

'Because it's very focused on the central area of the bubble, and our calculations indicate that I will travel one day forward, in the same relative position. I will reappear in the bubble twenty-three hours later. But you and Mom are going to Hawaii to be as far away as possible, just so you don't feel so worried. And I'll join you in a week. I'll need a vacation by then.'

Daddy kissed me as we got on the plane. 'Just in case,' he said.

*

Personally, I have no idea if Hawaii will be far enough away not to be affected if Daddy's force decides to concentrate on lots of mass being sent somewhere, instead of sending just Daddy a long way, or a long time. I don't understand his calculations very well.

Before we left, I asked Daddy if he was sure that the efficiency level stayed the same. 'Or could there be another like, trigger level, that makes it even more efficient? Or even two levels – and make the force even more super-efficient?'

He laughed. That wasn't very nice of him. 'Right,' he said, 'so I'll be spread all over the universe at once, and forward a billion years, hmm, Little Lady?'

'Or perhaps,' I said, 'the whole world will move somewhere else, or right into the future?'

He laughed again and told me not to worry. 'Natilie, I have every confidence that Zero 9-4 is absolutely precisely correct, and nothing unexpected can possibly occur.'

'But I do worry, Daddy. Just because I'm only twelve – and I'm a girl – it doesn't mean I can't think.' But he laughed again and gave me and Mom another goodbye kiss.

***

Anyway, if I've worked out the exact time difference between Daddy's laboratory in Boston and here in Waikiki, then I think they should be pressing the button about n—'

BY THE SAME AUTHOR

The definitive giant-sized anthology of thirty-nine highly entertaining and thought-provoking Sci-Fi short stories, some of which are selected from the books of the New-Classic series. Four hundred and forty pages filled with snappy two-pagers such as "Air Sacs and Frilly Bits" and "On the Seventh's Day" to the novella-length "The Colonist".

Could you keep ahead of "Melissa?", or manage an encounter "Of the 4th Kind"?

From the laughs of "I'm a Squumaid" to the tears of "The Twelve Days of Crystal-Ammas", these are the best and most varied stories in the universe – according to eleven alien species and the author's mum. With two Sci Fi poems, two adapted stories from the trilogy novels "Realms of Kyre" and "A Wisp of Stars" and twenty-five illustrations.

Published in eBook and Paperback in Feb 2020

BOOK TWO IN THE NEW-CLASSIC SCI-FI SERIES

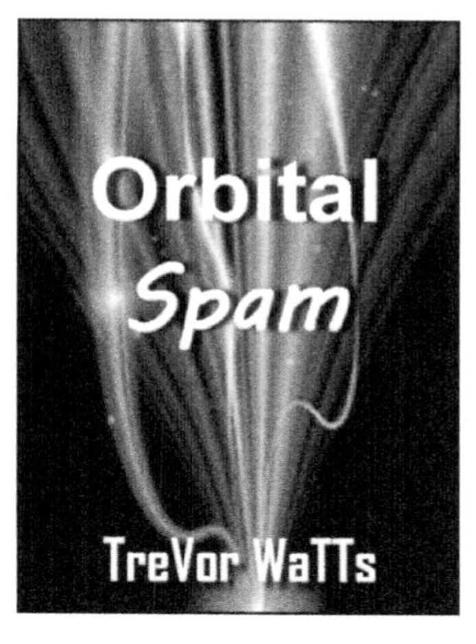

You've been dumped in the orbital spam folder, so what do you do about it, before the whole orbit is deleted?

What is it that's "Come Again" on the agricultural planet of Kalėdas, just when the seasonal workers and left-over troops are readying themselves to leave?

If you receive the "Prasap1" call, totally out the vac, are you going to answer it?

While concreting the base within the single-brick-high walls of the new pub, what are you going to do when a trail of disembodied footprints determinedly heads straight for you across the wet surface in "Self-Levelling"?

From the laughs of Puppetmaster, I Can Only Take So Much, and To Somercotes and Beyond, to the poignant stories of Yay-Hesh and Zydd, there, these 20+ brilliant tales will alter your view of the future that awaits, whether Out There, or here on Earth.

BOOK THREE IN THE NEW-CLASSIC SCI-FI SERIES

Twenty+ stories from the here and now, wondering what's hiding among us; to the far-strewn arms of the galaxy where humans exist no more.

When Prisoner 296 is sent to carry out repairs in the Khuk spaceport's entrance tunnel at rush hour, will he find out why it's known as The "Terminal Space"? What on Earth can the alien do when he's stuck, in "Traffic" and going to miss his spaceship home?

Could it be you who writes the heartfelt plea to Agony Aunt, Maar'juh'rih Ghruughs?

When it comes to that vital First Contact moment, would you have a better plan than "Polly", in the SS Stella Nova?

If it depended on you, would there "Always be an England"?

As Princess Porkyu said at the Cygnus Arms in 2929, "Laugh or catch your breath; shed a tear or cheer them on, you'll soar to the stars with these souls of the universe."

Printed in Great Britain
by Amazon

72866155R00129